VIPER

THE PROPHECY

Candi Fox

in collaboration with

Linny Lawless

Copyright © 2020 by Candi Fox

Cover design: pro_ebookcovers

Edited by: Lily Luchesi

Beta Reader: Sherri Short

Foxy Cheer Readers: Sherri Short & Dede Long
These two make your reading experience so much better.

Chapter 1

Viper

Headed up 75 toward home, he'd been on a mission for Omen and was headed back from Mexico City. He promised his mate he'd be back in time for the twins' birthday. Their boys would turn eighteen soon and experience their first shift.

While he'd hoped to find solid leads on the location of Odin's horn, at least he'd found some information and the corner of a map. He passed Dallas, only one hundred and eighteen miles to go until he was in the arms of the woman he loved.

Hard to believe it would be twenty years on October 13th. It seemed like only yesterday.

January 01, 2000

In three days, Logan Haagan would officially retire after serving twenty years on the Dallas police force. Even with magick to magickally age his appearance, a man his age should be slowing down physically. People already teased him about being in such good shape for an "old guy".

"Car 54, check out a 10-59 in the warehouse district, 1002 Ersel Street."

"10-4, dispatch. We'll check it out."

He pulled a U-turn, flipping on the sirens as they headed toward the warehouse district. The streets were nearly empty at half-past three in the morning. Less than ten minutes later he turned off the sirens, leaving on the lights while they cruised down the deserted lanes of the warehouse.

A wave of preternatural energy hit his senses long before they pulled up to the building address, dispatch gave them. *Fuck.* He would be stuck with a rookie tonight. Once out of the car he pulled his gun.

"Kincaid, follow me."

He didn't wait to see if the kid followed or not, he entered the building through a slightly opened door on the West side of the building. The copper scent of blood hit his nostrils as soon as he stepped through the door. He'd probably have to find a Mesmer to wipe the rookie's mind after tonight.

The sound of flesh hitting flesh unmistakable. There must be a magical barrier in place to mute the sound.

Using his superior night vision, he navigated around the hundreds of crates toward the center of the warehouse. As they drew nearer, he picked up dozens of smells. *Shit!* There must be a hundred bodies packed in here, and under a spell.

At least the rookie would make it out alive and he wouldn't have to erase his memories. Mesmers were pricey and he was saving for a gym of his own. Finally, he came to the center; peeking out from behind a large crate, he took in the scene.

His eyes scanned through the crowd until they found the center. To combatants in the ring. One large, green-skinned humanoid wearing a bone helmet with horns, a slayer, fought with the most beautiful woman he ever laid eyes on.

She had to be over six feet tall with long, lean muscles. Her thick dark hair pulled back into a ponytail. Both sides of her head shaved. She ducked and weaved as the slayer tried to use his horns to gore her.

"Haagan, all clear here."

"All clear."

Logan pulled a silver orb out of his pocket, his last time warp orb. He crushed it in his hand, turning back to watch the fight. He had twenty minutes before time affected him again. Slayers were nasty beasts created to kill and used by the criminal underworld as a hitman and hired by the unsavory as assassins. Their hide is as thick as a rhino and covered in thorns. Some of them over an inch long and nearly as hard as the mouth full of gleaming, razor-sharp teeth. Near seven feet in height, some topped out over eight feet tall.

The slayer charged the woman at the last-minute; changing trajectory, he was able to catch her in the ribs. Blood splattered as one of the smaller horns gored her side. She surprised him by grabbing onto the slayer's larger horns, pulling the smaller ones out of her side as she brought her knee up under her opponent's chin, she used the downward force hitting the slayer's jaw. He heard a loud crack. The slayer reared back in pain.

Logan watched the wound on the woman's side begin to scab over. She stepped a few feet away from her opponent before springing forward in a punch that nearly unhinged the slayer's broken jaw. The slayer slashed out, its claws slicing open the woman's arm in several places. More blood splattered in the ring and onto the surrounding audience.

The slayer pressed the advantage, snapping at the woman's throat with sharp, carnivorous teeth. She bent back, the teeth narrowly missing her. Her leg moved with lightning speed, kicking her opponent's knee in the soft tissue area. A move that rewarded her with distance from those deadly teeth.

She went back to dodging the slayer while her wounds started scabbing over. Not quite superhuman healing, but much faster than sleepers. During one of her dodges, the slayer grabbed a hold of her ponytail. He let go as quickly as he grabbed, blood dripping from the palm of his hand. The woman took advantage of his momentary distraction to deliver another punishing blow to her opponent's jaw. This hit should render his jaw useless unless slayers had gained super healing abilities, their ability lies in taking punishment.

This time she didn't step back. Her blows came swiftly and, if he wasn't mistaken, her fists seemed to take on the texture of the slayer's horns and head plate. A fist of solid bone pummeling the tough hide. The fast and furious blows enough to back the slayer in the corner. She continued to deliver punishing blows using her fists.

When the opportunity arose, she landed a blow to her opponent's knee loud enough to break it. No whistle blew, no referee in sight. She continued to reduce the slayer to a bloody pulp while taking blows of her own. Instead of backing away, she pressed on. Eventually, the slayer stopped moving. The crowd started yelling, "Occidere! Occidere!"

He quickly searched his brain while watching the woman. The word meant 'kill' in Latin.

She shook her head, "He's unconscious and cannot continue. I win. If you want him killed, do your own dirty work, Cayum."

A Dark Fae stood, his milky white skin shining like pale moonlight. He regarded the woman in the ring before walking toward the stage. The crowd of preternatural beings parted, leaving plenty of space for the Fae and his bodyguards to get to the makeshift ring. He jumped over the ropes and walked to the woman reaching for her arm. He held it aloft.

"Lady Death for the win. World Championship number nine for those of you counting."

The crowd went wild drowning out any more words. Even with his superior hearing. They cheered so loud it shook the building.

He kept his eyes on the pair in the center of the ring. Neither looked happy, though it was tough to tell through all the blood and bruises blooming on the woman's face. Lady Death, he'd heard about her for the last decade. A newcomer that took the underground fighting world by storm at the young age of sixteen.

Once the crowd calmed down the Dark Fae started speaking again.

"In a surprising turn of events, Lady Death announces this is her last fight. What a way to go out on top! Nine times in a row, something that's never been done before."

Logan could tell the Fae named Cayum was less than thrilled about Lady Death's retirement, but he hid it well and amped up the crowd.

This time, after the crowd died down, the people started collecting money or paying the bookies before they exited the building. One thing you never squelched on was a bet with a paranormal bookie. Some bookies, normally those associated with the Tromluí, the Dark Fae's equivalent of the mafia, had witches put up death wards. No matter how big you lost, you paid the bookie. Money, flesh, part of your soul, or some task to be named later. If you didn't you died, or worse.

The 'worse' got Logan thinking it was high time he put away the badge and started running with Odin's Wolves again.

Technically they were one-percenters, however; he liked to see them more as the Punisher.

A group of godlike wolf shifters, warriors with centuries of training and combat. He could take on pieces of shit like Cayum. Once he saw the woman safely leave, he popped back into time.

"Nothing to report, let's go call dispatch."

The rest of the shift went by uneventfully. He stopped at a diner before heading home. Logan spent the next several hours making phone calls. First to Omen, to let him know he'd be turning in his notice and heading to White Horse, OK. The second call to Mother, the club's techno mage. He could enter the internet and get into the dark web. Logan wanted information on the Dark Fae he saw last night. He had a hunch the male was nothing but trouble.

Chapter 2

Death

"That was a big mistake, Billie, your little friend Ava is going to be auctioned off to the highest bidder."

Billie Cameron straightened her spine. At two inches above six feet, she towered over Cayum. Not that size mattered. The Dark Fae was both vicious and powerful. She knew better than to underestimate him. She thought about her next move, she wanted to punch him in the throat and leave, but she wasn't stupid.

She hated the motherfucker, just like she hated all men. Men were nothing but lying pieces of shit that wanted to own you or use you. Except one, the man in her dreams. The one that saved her and taught her how to fight.

Her life might have been different had she trusted him and took his offer for help, instead of disappearing. Hiding is her specialty. Something she did better than anyone else. Even better than fighting.

She may have worked for Cayum, but the fights were real. Her skill was real, and right now she was in a real pickle. You see, Ava was already safe, where even she didn't know. She had to get to White Horse, Oklahoma, and find a man that went by the name Devil. He would know where Ava was being kept.

"I'm done killing for you, Cayum. I won nine straight titles. Our deal is done. You never said I had to kill the slayer."

"You knew I would expect it."

"But you didn't say it."

"Technicality, Miss Cameron. You owe me everything."

"I'm done, Cayum. No free for all for you."

"Do not challenge my authority! Your debts have not yet been paid."

She curled her nails into the palms of her hands, digging them into her flesh to keep from saying what she badly wanted to say.

"I'm not trying to challenge your authority. The slight wasn't intentional." She lied smoothly.

Suspicion and doubt were written all over Cayum's face. She could see the wheels turning in his mind.

"My contract said nine titles. I have nine titles."

Cayum grins. "I hope you don't plan on leaving Dallas anytime soon, Miss Cameron. You should think about poor little Ava. She's so very precious and a fine commodity."

"Are you going to give her to me next week or not?"

"That all depends on you. Give me your word right now Billie, that you will not leave Dallas until I say you can."

"Fine, I give you my word. I won't leave Dallas until you say I can. I've got no place to go anyway. Since we live on the road. No home to speak of. Dallas is as good a place as any other."

Thinking she got lucky, she walked away planning her next move.

Cayum

He watched her walk away. He wasn't done with her, not by a long shot. Billie Cameron, aka Lady Death, was a gold mine and he had no plans to let her go. Taking the phone out of his pocket, he dialed one of the witches he had on contract.

"Maeve, I have a job for you. I need a tracer on Lady Death. I need to know if she goes outside city limits."

He hung up the phone, not waiting for a reply.

Cayum was going to stay one step ahead of Billie. He would keep feeding her the lies of what he was going to do with Ava.

Maeve was one of his top-notch witches and Cayum knew the minute he hung up the phone the trace on Billie was already in the works.

Death

She let out a sigh of relief, knowing she only had a short window to get the hell out of dodge. Cayum no doubt had some kind of tail on her. She could spot one of his goons miles away, he would know that, which means he hired out. The question was, who?

There was a slim chance he wouldn't find out Ava was missing for a few days. A less than one percent chance if memory served her correctly.

Beautiful scrollwork covered most of her right side, hiding a nasty scar, just missing her breast, and ending at her hip. Cayum hired one of her opponents to gut her, only Billie dodged; surprising everyone by sprouting the same blade-type protrusions, taking off the guy's head as he cut down her side.

She had no idea how she did it that fast. At that time, she had yet to master her mimic ability. Billie had no control over when it worked or how long it lasted. Some instinct to survive must have kicked in, expediting her reactions allowing her to kill her opponent before she passed out from blood loss.

It took her six weeks to heal enough from her injuries to get back in the ring. The fight was a turning point in her miserable life. She started killing for Cayum after that. Later, when she couldn't stomach killing one more being, he showed her Ava. He told her that he'd have the girl raped and beaten while she watched. All Billie had to do to stop it was to continue to do what she did best: kill.

With the scar to remind her what would happen if she didn't do his bidding, Lady Death was born. A little piece of her died with each death. Billie secretly performed burial rites for each opponent she had to kill. Most of the time, Cayum didn't bother with the bodies after he took his piece for the trophy room.

She couldn't go back to that, and she wouldn't have to. Time and money helped grease the wheels for her escape. Billie started the Harley; her baby should be as safe as Ava by now unless she misplaced her trust. The man's name *is* Devil. Knowing Cayum would love to get his hand on the custom bike she created, the entire bike had been built and stored. Billie had yet to set eyes on it.

Living on the streets taught her many life lessons, including who you could trust and who you could pay to keep your secrets. Cayum found her a few months before her sixteenth birthday, tired and hungry. She'd been drawn to the man; at the time she didn't know he glamoured her.

Billie hadn't known enough to understand what Cayum had done to her until it was too late. She only experienced odd flashes of power when she needed to defend herself or protect the weaker.

Most of the time she wrote it off as a freaky coincidence. No matter how many times it happened, Billie was never convinced.

You had to be someone special to have those kinds of powers; she was no one special.

By the time she realized Cayum's evil intentions, it was too late. He played her well. She owed him for the clothes on her back, the roof over her head, and the food in her stomach. Billie tried to get out of his grip, each time she only wound up deeper in his debt. It was time to break away once and for all.

Pulling out her phone she dialed one of her contacts.

"It's a go."

"On it."

With time to kill, she pulled into a gas station, topping off the tank. The timing had to be perfect if she was going to pull this off. Besides, killing a few hours driving around the city would help her detect any goons Cayum might have sent to keep an eye on her.

Billie pulled onto the nearly empty highway. In a few hours, traffic would start to pick up as the early shift went in and the graveyard shift started home from work. At that time, she hoped to make her escape from the city.

Her mind wandered, and she tried to imagine what it would feel like to be truly free of Cayum's sinister control. It was something she never felt before, nor dreamed of, since it always felt unreachable.

Living on the streets as a small child, Billie constantly had to be on guard from predators of various sorts. Just like the saying goes: "sleep with one eye open" was exactly the way Billie lived day in day out.

Chapter 3

Viper

Logan pulled out the photos from a large manilla envelope. Dozens of black and white photos of his current obsession. A courier delivered it a few moments ago. He should have tried to sleep, but he couldn't. He needed to know who Lady Death was and what the Dark Fae mafia was up to. Even though he planned on heading to White Horse as soon as he retired, he could still give the local shifter community a heads up.

Not to mention she seemed familiar. A memory niggled at the back of his mind; he knew her. They had some former connection, maybe a past life of hers. He would remember meeting a woman like her. Over six feet of beauty and fine toned muscle. Deadly grace. His cock twitched thinking of her finely honed body, not to mention that ass.

I bet I could bounce a quarter off that tight ass. He wanted to do a whole lot more to it. Yeah, he had it bad. The mere thought had his cock standing at attention. Good thing he didn't have to walk anywhere for a while. He turned on the radio laughing out loud when Sisquo's 'Thong Song' came on. Logan had zero doubts her ass would look hella delicious in a thong.

He studied each photo; the majority were inside of a fighting ring. Many of them over the body of a dead opponent. At least he knew how she got her notorious nickname. His phone rang. Logan flipped open the Motorola Razr.

"Haagen here."

"You sure the Dark Fae's name is Cayum?"

"That's what she said."

"Fuck! When are you heading this way?"

"Why, what's up?"

"Cayum is Capo for the Tromluí."

"Fuck, I might need back up."

"I have a contact down there; she goes by Nightingale. I'll give you her number, she's expecting your call."

"Let me grab a pen. Got it."

"214-698-2931. I'll see you in two."

"Thanks, brother, catch you on the flip."

"See that you do."

Logan understood what the club's VP, Blade, meant. Dark Fae could be nasty to deal with on any day, add the Tromluí and you had a recipe for a disaster of epic proportions. The Tromluí were the Dark Fae's mafia. A nasty organization with the power to make you wish you were dead. They believed death was the easy way out.

The question foremost on his mind, how deep was Lady Death into the organization, or what did the capo have hanging over her head?

Logan quickly dialed the number Blade gave him.

"Hello."

"Is this Nightingale?"

"Who's asking?"

"Blade sent me."

"Meet me at Annie's off 75 in an hour."

"How will I find you?"

"I'll find you."

She disconnected the call. His night was turning into a bad action flick. Mysterious calls, Fae mafia, and a woman he couldn't get out of his mind.

Logan took a long, hot shower and didn't bother to shave after. He planned on growing a beard. He doubted the Captain would bust him for scruff with the time he had left.

With plenty of time left to get to his destination, he twisted the throttle wide open on his bike and headed down 35. What's the worst that could happen, he'd get a ticket? With a wicked grin, he sped on topping 90 MPH. He loved seeing the city fly by. While Dallas always had traffic this time of the morning, he could easily maneuver through it without the need to stop or slow down.

He couldn't wait for true freedom, the open road, and no boss to report to. Logan didn't have to join the police force, but through the decades he felt drawn to be on the force or in the military. He didn't mind the structure, what he loved was serving the greater good, helping people.

Now that didn't mean he was a pushover or a goody-two-shoes. Logan liked to think of himself more like the Punisher. You couldn't always take out the trash within the legal limits of the law. Logan had no problem crossing the line for the right reason. He served his own form of justice when it was needed.

He arrived fifteen minutes early, the place about half full. Annie's, one of the twenty-four-hour diners that served the Metropolitan area, was one of his favorite hangouts. Not many cops hung out here, but plenty of bikers did. Since he was in plain clothes most of the time, he didn't have to worry about it. He wasn't even supposed to be on the last shift; he'd filled in when a few too many of his brothers called in with the blue flu.

A middle-aged waitress with a kind smile and tired eyes showed him to a back booth, per his request. He wanted to sit with his back to the wall and his eyes on everything else. The waitress rushed back, placing a table mat, silverware, and a glass of ice water down before handing him the menu.

"I'll be right back to take your food order, hun. Can I get you anything else to drink?"

"I'll take a cherry shake, add hot fudge. Make that two, and I'd love a pitcher of water."

"Sure thing. I'll be right back with that water."

"Thank you," he looked at her name tag, "Flo."

As soon as Flo disappeared behind the counter, a young woman slid into the booth in front of him. Her long lavender hair spilling out from a dark hood.

"Nightingale."

Deep lilac eyes met his, while her face looked like a young twenty-something human, her eyes held the weight of the ages. Her oversized hood no doubt hid her delicate, pointed ears.

"Viper."

"Are you hungry?"

"Always." She smiled.

He laughed. "Food's on me. Have whatever you want."

Her eyes danced with merriment. "I will, thank you."

The waitress came back with a second menu, table setup, and his shake.

"Is that a cherry shake with hot fudge?"

Flo smiled at his new companion. "It sure is, sugar. Would you like one?

"She can have mine; I'll take a double with my meal."

"Sure thing, should I give you a few minutes?"

Nightingale answered, "I'm ready if he is."

"Ladies first."

"I'll take the chunky monkey stuffed French toast, cherry supreme pancakes, candied apple pecan waffle, and a large glass of chocolate milk. Oh, and for dessert, I want a hot fudge sundae with extra cherries."

"What can I get for you, sir?"

"I'll take three double cheeseburgers medium, mayo, mustard, and ketchup only, and a double large order of bacon cheese fries add nacho cheese and extra bacon."

Flo didn't bat an eye at the outrageous order the two placed. She scribbled it all down heading off with the promise to come back with the chocolate milk.

"I hear you're looking into Cayum. Before I answer your questions, I need to know why."

He opened the link to his wolf allowing him to take over all his human senses. Logan tuned into the immediate area around them, making sure it was clear before pulling a small metal device out of his pocket. It resembled a small flat desk bell with no clinker. Once activated the device would prevent anyone from overhearing from preternatural means, it would also protect the sleepers around them by emitting a low frequency. The pitch caused sleepers to "tune-out" or mishear the conversation. Like playing the telephone game.

When he pressed the top flush with the lower body a pop of energy hummed to life making his skin tingle. The fairly common device shouldn't draw preternatural attention. After all, the preternatural world remained hidden. Most people had no idea they worked beside shifters, vampires, and other "mythological" creatures on a daily/nightly basis.

Great pains were taken to see their world would remain under wraps. The sleepers weren't anywhere near ready to know Dracula not only lived, but he's probably banged ninety-nine percent of Hollywood by now; or that most of the celebrities that died young were part of the community. Tough to hide that whole not aging thing. One of the reasons he'd spent most of his career undercover; full beards hid a youthful face.

"I'm interested in his connection with Lady Death."

Nightingale brightened; he could almost see her ears twitch with anticipation.

"You like her."

"I'm interested in knowing more about her."

"Here you are," Flo interrupted them, sitting their drinks on the table, before unloading the rest of the serving tray and two more. How she managed to make it all fit on the table, he'd never know.

"You two need anything else?"

"We're good for now, thanks," he replied.

Nightingale waited until the waitress walked away to dive into the proverbial dirt.

"Cayum is Capo on the Tromluí. He's in town recruiting for the fights. Lady Death wasn't supposed to win the fight. Cayum didn't want her dead or permanently injured. He wanted her to have to start the count over again for his deal with her. Billie Cameron's her name, by the way."

Logan absorbed the information watching in awe as the petite Fae managed to eat and talk at the same time without food tumbling out or mumbling her words.

"If she won nine titles in a row, something never done before, then he had to release her from her contract."

"How did she get involved in the first place?"

"It's her story to tell, but I'll say this: she was young, and he tricked her."

"Why is he intent on keeping her, when there are so many willing to fight?"

"Because she can do what no one else has been able to do, she's the best fighter he's ever had. You can bet he won't let her go that easy."

He knew the moment she walked into the diner. Not wanting to give his interest away, Logan tracked her location by scent as she took a seat in another corner booth. The fates had surely smiled on him this day.

"Cayum's as dangerous as they come. He will do whatever it takes to get her back under this thumb. He'll kill anyone that gets in his way."

"Duly noted. What else can you tell me?"

"That you should stay away from him."

"The chances of that happening are dwindling rapidly."

"Cayum is well connected and has powerful Dark Fae magic. I've never seen any being escape his wrath without begging to be forever destroyed."

"Suggestions on how to deal with him?"

"Avoidance."

He laughed, "Besides avoidance?"

"It depends on what you want. Contact a broker or moderator if you cannot avoid making his acquaintance."

He paid the bill, leaving Flo a generous tip. The magic device back in his pocket he sat outside on his bike as false dawn began to light the sky.

Chapter 4

Death

She felt the pull of dawn long before she walked outside. With enough time to lose herself in morning traffic and make her rendezvous, she missed the man watching her from his bike. The Harley fired up with a purr, Billie headed back onto 75.

Traffic filled every lane of the highway beginning to slow as morning rush hour started. Billie chose the middle lanes, hoping to be able to maneuver through traffic easier. After hitting a snarl, she needed to make up time heading to the outer lane she wove through the dense traffic before hitting an open spot in the road.

Billie opened the throttle up, hitting the speed limit before pushing the bike faster. Her need to get out of town before Cayum found out Ava was not in his grasp anymore made her throw caution to the wind and blow past the speed limit.

It took her at least a minute before she heard the siren behind. *Fuck, I do not need this.* Billie started to pull over; looking through her rearview mirror, she saw the cop wave her over. She maneuvered over to the emergency lane about half a mile from the next exit.

Billie pulled her helmet off watching the officer pull his bike over, surprised it wasn't a police issue bike.

Viper

He followed her down the highway easily, and when her speed reached over ninety, he knew he had good reason to pull her over.

Viper needed to meet her in person. He needed to know what this inexplicable draw was.

Logan watched her watch his approach, her body language relaxed. She gave him the once over by the time he reached her side. He pulled out his badge.

"Do you know how fast you were going?"

"95."

"Is there some emergency you needed to get to?"

"Just heading out of town."

"Like your tail has been set on fire. Running away from something or someone?"

"Look, give me the speeding ticket and let me go."

"Impatient much?"

He watched her nostrils flare with impatience. *She's quite the spitfire, I approve.*

"Are you going to give me a ticket or not?"

"Depends."

She stopped mid-speech, looking at him as if trying to figure out his angle. He could tell she immediately made up her mind to hate him. *Damn,* he'd have to switch tactics.

"Let me guess, I give you a blow job or something and you let me go? You wouldn't be the first cop to say something like that."

He had the grace to look abashed; he wasn't going to ask for sex, but he did want her phone number.

"Honestly, I was going to ask for your phone number. That's not why I pulled you over."

"You pulled me over because I was doing ninety-five in a seventy. I suppose I'll give you my number and you'll let me out of the ticket?"

"Tell me why you're really in a hurry to get out of town."

She didn't have that nasty glare of impatience anymore. She crossed her arms over her chest. "How is that any of your business? Just give me the ticket."

Logan handed his ticket pad and pen to her. "How about you scribble your phone number here, and I give you a warning this time?"

She rolled her eyes, but he could tell she struggled not to smile as she took the pad and wrote her phone number down.

By the time they finished their conversation, the skies turned black, lightning cracked in through the air. He could smell the storm coming.

"Better get out of the rain. It's going to be a bad storm."

She glared at him before she started her bike and took off. Knowing she was most likely running for her life; he had the suspicious feeling she would try to ride out the storm no matter how dangerous it became.

He let out a sigh before starting his bike and following after her.

Death

Late didn't even begin to describe her current situation; she needed to make it to White Horse, to the safe house. Then she could think about her next step. Ava, her custom bike, and freedom awaited her. First, she needed to get to the state border. In five minutes, she'd be out of Dallas and hopefully put some more distance between her and Cayum's goons.

Once she was inside of the safehouse, she would be free of him and any witches he decided to send after her. The rain started as a drizzle. She kept the speed limit but did more weaving in and out of traffic to make sure she didn't stop again.

Five miles outside of Dallas, she knew two things. One, the cop was still following her, and two, the pit of dread in her stomach told her Cayum knew something. It would be a matter of time before one or more of his goons caught up with her.

She only hoped her head start would help. The rain turned from a drizzle into a steady pour. People being stupid, as usual, started to hydroplane in the downpour. Oil often came to the surface at the beginning of heavy rainfall.

Her superior reflexes kept her out of half a dozen accidents. Her speed slowed to fifty, she needed the extra two seconds to avoid the idiots. Glancing in her rearview mirror, she spotted the cop. He was a persistent motherfucker. A hot, persistent mother fucker.

Billie rarely gave into her libido, but there was something about him that made her want to rip both of their clothes off. She struggled with the attraction not fully understanding it,

good thing he wouldn't be sticking around. She had no doubt they'd be naked and breathing heavily in no time flat.

He reacted to her the same way, she reacted to him. Only she perfected the perfect poker face for most of her life. On top of that, something niggled at the back of her mind, some memory. He seemed familiar to her, yet she hadn't met him until he pulled her over. Detective Logan Haagan according to his I.D., if he hadn't shown it to her she would have left. The guy had a siren, but no uniform and an unmarked bike. One that looked suspiciously like a civi bike, nothing law enforcement would use.

He pissed her off by making her late, admittedly it pissed her off, even more that she wanted to fuck him on the 75 during rush hour traffic. Had her brain suddenly turned cro magnon? Fuck, feed, survive. He somehow represented all three of those basic instincts, and that threw her more than anything, which made her angrier.

Instinctively, she knew he was something more than a sleeper. Preternatural energy rolled off him in thick waves. Yet another thing that made zero sense. Alpha males of all varieties and species surrounded her daily. Shifters, vampires, creatures, and monsters. Things spliced together by magic. Things of horror.

That last thought shifted her focus just enough that she managed to avoid being hit by a truck swerving into her lane by less than six inches. Her breath held as she watched the truck tailspin out of control, and it collided with another truck that collided with the car in the next lane. She glanced back and forth to the road around her before checking the rearview. The cop hadn't emerged yet. Did he stop or was he dead?

She should go back and check. *NO!* Cayum would surely find her if she went back. *Fuck, fuck, fuck, fuck!* Billie had to do something. Using her finely honed senses she spotted an emergency roadside phone a mile up the road. Increasing her speed, she made a beeline for the phone.

After a quick anonymous tip on the crash with possible officer involvement, she headed back on the road. The rain pelted down mercilessly now. She wondered if Cayum had it conjured. Cars, trucks, and other bikes were pulling over, unable to navigate any farther.

Billie knew she couldn't stop, she had to keep going. Drawing in a deep breath, she narrowed her focus down to her immediate surroundings, tight enough she had time to react, not so large as to draw unwanted attention in case one of her hidden abilities decided to show up. She possibly picked up something from the cop.

Normally her mimic abilities only kicked in when she was fighting. A defense mechanism of sorts, honestly, she had no freakin' clue how they worked. On rare occasions, she picked up an ability by being in physical contact with them. It happened three times previously. Each time her life had been in mortal danger and each time her ability kicked in, saving her life.

In the span of a heartbeat, she knew her time to run had come to an end. Familiar energy signatures pinged at her sixth sense. Her only chance now lay in her ability to hide. One that never failed her.

Billie twisted the throttle on the bike, picking up as much speed as she dared. She sent the bike toward a light post waiting until the last nanosecond possible; she jumped off the bike. It took less than five seconds for the impact of the road to burn through her leathers and hit her skin. Excruciating pain flared through every nerve ending in her body before the slayer's rhino-like hide formed over her bare skin.

She lay in a ditch, naked, shivering from cold and fear, trying to slow her breath enough to enact her innate hiding abilities. Time slowed down as she fought with her breath, her heart beating like a drum in her ears with each exhale. Cayum's goons were less than a thousand yards away from her. Pulling in her energy as rapidly as possible, she didn't have time to detect what direction they were coming from.

One of them caught her energy signature. She pulled her energy in faster; she would be "shut down", untraceable. Seeing no other choice, she hit the "big red button" in her consciousness that would force an immediate shutdown. Billie had only done it one other time, she lost three months while her body rebooted. Her last thoughts were on Ava before she floated in limbo. Velvety liquid darkness surrounded her.

Last time she'd been exhausted and simply relaxed into the void allowing her consciousness to "sleep" while her body recovered. This time she didn't have that luxury. She drew in a deep breath, allowing her senses to fill with warm golden light, expelling the liquid darkness from her body. Billie repeated the exercise twice more before her body began to awaken. She lay perfectly still, listening, and nothing more.

Chapter 5

Viper

He managed to avoid crashing his bike when the truck caused the multi-car pile-up. *Duty first.* Logan pulled over at the underpass pulling out the police issued phone/2-way radio he called in the accident before heading to the scene to see what he could do to help.

The wreck reminded him of a scene in Vietnam, bodies, and parts of bodies strewn around the road, glass, blood, and the screams of pain from the injured and dying.

Odin keep her safe until I can be again by her side. He sent up a quick prayer to the All-Father before starting triage.

He looked to the stopped cars behind him first. Pulling his badge from his pocket he used an alpha trick to project his voice. "I'm Detective Logan Haagan with the Dallas Police Department. I need anyone with medical experience or medical supplies to please come forward. Medical supplies include medical kits, blankets, tarps, extra clothes, cloth to use for bandages.

"I've contacted dispatch and units are already on their way. If we work together, we can save lives. I also need coolers, chests, and ice. Lots of ice. The city can reimburse anyone if need be."

Four hours later with dry clothes, thank Odin the rain stopped, he was on his way to find Billie Cameron. Officially retired thanks to his "heroic" efforts at the accident. All he did was organize everyone, bitch slap an idiot or two, and help a woman deliver her fifth child.

Before he left the underpass, he called forth his wolf, allowing his superior senses to take over. Once he adjusted to the shift, he started down the road. Six months of daily practice and dozens of broken bones later, his wolf learned to 'drive' the motorcycle. An invaluable trick, well worth every bruise and taunt he took from his brothers. *He missed those sons of bitches.*

Odin smile on him, perhaps Billie's path took her toward his brothers. Toward home, in this case, White Horse, Oklahoma. It changed every half-century or so. The wolves tended to go where they were most needed. Omen, their leader, President of the OWMC. Odin's Wolves foresaw the need to be in White Horse for the awakening.

When the awakening would come, he did not know. Rage, their sergeant at arms, moved to White Horse a few years ago to set up base; along with a few of his other brothers. He looked forward to helping build their new home base.

A few miles up the road he picked up her scent.

His heart clenched when he spotted the wreckage of her bike. A quick search told him she didn't die here. Logan paused looking until he found the skid marks. After seeing her expertly handle the bike in the down pouring rain, he didn't think anything could have caused her to wreck.

Concentrating, he closed out the world around him, his sole focus on finding her.

Death

The cop hit her senses as soon as she became consciously aware. Taking a few more precious seconds she felt around for Cayum's goons before she opened her eyes and sat up. After a few disorienting seconds she spotted Logan a hundred yards away.

Billie looked around, pinpointing a couple of rocks. She wanted to get his attention and not half the highways. Using only the movement necessary, she threw a stone at him. He looked up, on the second one, and caught her eye by the third. She lay back down praying he didn't say get up or some cop bullshit.

Moments later she looked up into concerned blue eyes. He took his jacket off, bending down to help wrap her in it, and scooping her up into his arms in a matter of seconds. The swiftness of the movements made her head spin. Pushing her body to wake up after a reset would cost her. She only hoped it didn't cost her, her life.

"You can explain later. Right now, I'm going to get you on my bike to someplace safe. I'm sorry to say nothing on your bike survived."

"I didn't expect it to, thanks for looking."

"I found it first."

She nodded her head. "Thanks for looking for me. Why did you?"

"Another thing we can talk about once I get you to safety."

Viper

He made use of his large frame to shield her from prying eyes as he carried her to his bike. Once there he pulled out a small emergency blanket he kept under the seat.

"Let me wrap this around you. Do you think you can hold on to me?"

"I'm not sure."

He removed the bungee cords he had strapped to the bike, "I can carry you; we'll go a little slower, is all."

She offered him a smile before laying her head on his shoulder. Her eyes closed, her breathing even before he started the bike. Viper carefully wrapped the bungee cords around both, securing Billie's body to his.

Cradling her against his chest, he balanced their weight and took off, staying in the slow lane in case he needed to get off quickly. Instead of taking either of the first two exits, he chose to take the third. A friend of his had a small cabin not far from the state line. He'd been hunting with him on several occasions. Devil wouldn't mind him dropping in unannounced.

Twenty-five minutes later, he pulled the bike down a well-maintained gravel road to a small one-bedroom cabin. The cabin looked to be in disrepair, but Logan knew it was only a Fae charm. A larger, four-bedroom hunting cabin lay beyond the glamour.

A massive white wolf bounded down the step ready to pounce on him. Storm must have scented Billie at the last second, twisting his body to land beside Logan rather than pouncing him to the ground. The massive beast landed rather ungracefully.

"Thank you, buddy," he said, hoping to soothe the wolf's ego.

Storm gave a quick low growl in reply before getting up and trotting away head held high in the air.

"Viper?"

"Aye, I have a visitor."

"I see that," Devil said, appearing from behind a tree. His brother's piercing blue eyes met his, over Billie's unconscious form.

"What happened?"

"I'm not entirely sure. She didn't stay awake long enough to tell me what happened. I know she crashed her motorcycle before the state line, and she's probably being chased by the Tromluí."

Devil quirked a brow, his full mouth turning into a smile. "I smell a fight coming on. Come inside. Tell me more. I'll call Synne."

"Good idea, thanks, bro."

"I got you, plus. I mean you brought a good fight to my door, one that includes some delicious Dark Fae pussy."

"Do you think about anything besides sex and violence?

"Let me think." A plethora of expressions ran across his friend's face. "Nope, not a damn thing. Let's get that delicious package inside."

Viper's wolf rose to the surface rapidly bearing elongated teeth as his brother a low warning growl emitted from his throat.

"Oh, testy. Viper's got a girlfriend. You know what that means, right?"

"No, you will not say that corny line again."

"It will happen."

A cocky grin on his face, Devil turned and strolled into the cabin. Viper shook his head; motherfucker was going to do it. Billie shivered in his arms as they passed through the wards of the hunting cabin. The energy washing over them, enveloping them, and hiding their trail.

The cabin doubled as a safe house in time of need. He'd know how much protection they needed once Billie awakened. Unless Synne knew something. Synne, a Dark Fae princess, tended to have her fingers in all the pies. If anyone would know more about Cayum it would be her.

He had a feeling Nightingale knew a lot more and wondered at her reluctance to get involved. If she didn't want to divulge information, she wouldn't have agreed to meet. Unless she was feeling him out for the Tromluí. Logan didn't think so, but stranger things have happened.

He carried her across the threshold, up the stairs to the double doors at the end of the hall. Devil rarely slept in the master suite when he stayed here preferring the bedroom on the lower floor in case, he had a midnight assignation. The man loved to fuck.

Logan carried her to the bed, balancing her on one knee long enough to pull down the covers. After tucking her in, he headed downstairs to meet his brother in the kitchen. Devil handed him a steaming hot mug of black coffee as soon as he stepped foot into the kitchen.

"Thank Odin. I needed this."

"I heard you're retiring and heading to White Horse."

"That was the plan."

"Was?"

"Depends on what's happening with Billie."

"Is she your mate?"

"I don't know. It doesn't feel like the mating bond, but I'm drawn to her, nonetheless. Something about her seems familiar, like I should know her. I keep thinking it's a past life. I mean, no way I wouldn't remember meeting her in this lifetime."

The devil laughed. "True, from what I did see, she's unforgettable."

His wolf seemed content with his brother's jesting assessment of his; whatever the hell she is to him. Odin only knew. Perhaps Omen would know something.

"Brother, is Omen at base?"

"No, he's out searching for the horn. Though he's due to check in later this week. I don't know if he will call in or show up, but he always checks in on time."

Chapter 6

Viper

"Good, I need some advice."

A soft shimmering blue portal appeared behind Devil. Viper didn't know what to think of the creature that walked out of the portal. The breathtaking, dark-skinned beauty smiled at him before pulling his brother in for a kiss.

"Synne, this is Viper. Viper, Synne."

Viper took her hand, bringing her knuckles to his lips and he softly brushed the back of them.

"I've not met Fae royalty before."

"Or from the looks of your face, a Dark Fae without milky white skin."

His smile genuine, he replied, "I admit I've heard rumors about shadow blessed Dark Fae. I thought they were stories until now."

Viper studied her for a moment, her skin dark and rich like freshly turned soil made her unusual blue eyes glow. Her dark hair twisted into twin-buns, silver and diamond earrings graced her delicately pointed ears.

"Do you have a cup of coffee for me, lover?

"I do."

"Make it Irish. Come into the living room, we can chat there. Is the girl still out?"

"Yes, she's asleep in the master bedroom."

"I'd like to check in on her after we talk."

"Sure."

Viper sat in a large, overstuffed chair leaving the sofa for Synne and Devil. His brother carried in two cups of coffee handing one to Synne before settling in beside her.

"Let's get the easy info out of the way, what's sleeping beauty's name?"

"Billie Cameron, she goes by the name Lady Death."

Synne whistled low before a wide grin split her face. "Boy, are you lucky, and unlucky, at the same time."

"Care to explain that?"

"Devil and I have a contract with her. I can't go into details without her permission. I will say that there is a safe place within the clubhouse I've prepared for her. If Cayum is looking for her, your best bet is to get her there."

He addressed Synne first, "Can you use the portal? Brother why didn't you tell me?"

"He's never seen her before. I did all the meetings, and I think it's too risky if he's looking for her. The longer my involvement remains under wraps, the better chance we have of keeping everyone safe. I can buy us some time. Do you have any idea what happened to her?"

"No clue."

"Let me check her out. I'll see if there is anything, I can do to get her up and running, so to speak. The wards on this place will buy you some time, but not forever. Not with Cayum involved."

"Understood."

Viper got up, leading the way up the stairs to the master bedroom. Billie lay on her side in a deep slumber, not stirring when he turned on the lamp. Synne holding her hands about six inches away from Billie's sleeping form, ran her hands all over.

"Her energy feels depleted. She's running on empty."

"Can we do an energy exchange?"

"We can send her enough energy to jump start her. I'm not sure what she needs. I've never come across anything like it. In addition to her battery being depleted, she has a tracer spell on her. Most likely someone Cayum hired, or strong-armed."

"How long do we have until they find her?"

"The wards will buy us a few hours. I have to be careful. I'm willing to help but don't want to start a war between the Royal Court and the Tromluí. Once she's safe in White Horse, I can openly play a larger role."

"I understand. Thanks for your help. How do we do this?"

"I want you both to imagine energy forming into a large ball in your hands. See it, feel it. When the ball gets to the size of a bowling ball, push it into Billie."

Viper concentrated feeling the energy, then picturing it growing in his hands. The ball grew to twice the size of a bowling ball before he released it, pushing into her body.

Death

Energy shot through her like a bolt of lightning, setting her nerve endings on fire. Relighting them like you would a pilot light. Her eyes flew open and she sat up, immediately going into a defensive position when she realized three bodies surrounded her and she had no idea where she was.

"Billie, you're safe. Remember I found you on the side of the highway?"

She relaxed slightly, taking in the cop and his two friends. The other man, shorter than Viper, had the kind of good looks that drive women wild. When he smiled at her, showing even white teeth and a dimple to die for, she automatically put him in the "do not take serious" category. She had a sneaking suspicion that he loved women as much as they loved him. Not her type. Did she have a type? She'd had sex a couple of times. Nothing to write home about if she had someone to write or a home.

The memories of the last several hours came flooding back. She jumped off the bed and threw her arms around the cop kissing him on the cheek, in a rare, impulsive move.

"I thought you bit it in the crash."

"I got skillz."

She went to withdraw her arms from around him realizing that his thick muscular arms were still wrapped around her. She panicked for a split second. He must have sensed her change as his arms dropped to his side. She blushed, stepping back.

"Glad to see you're alive."

"Thanks for the lift. I really need to go. I have someplace to be."

"How are you going to get there?"

"Fuck, the bike's trashed isn't it?"

"So are your clothes."

"Double fuck. I need to be gone."

"Before Cayum finds you?"

"Yes, plus I'm supposed to meet someone. I'm already late. I hope that I can still get there."

"Who are you supposed to meet?"

While she understood he was trying to help she bristled at the questioning. Her life is on the line, she didn't have time to chat. "It doesn't matter. If you will at least let me borrow a phone, I can call a few contacts and get out of your hair."

"Why don't you boys go make some food? I can hear her stomach rumble from here. I'll get her some clothes, and we'll be right down."

She waited until the boys left. "Thank you for the help, but I still need to get out of here."

"I know. I'm Synne the Fae helping you keep Ava safe. Devil is the slightly shorter male with lips to die for. The bigger one is Viper."

"With that grin, I can see why they call him Devil. How did Viper get his road name?"

Synne snickered. "Ask him or, better yet, ask Devil. I promise you won't be disappointed. I have some clothes here. With a little Fae magick, I can adjust them to fit you."

"How's Ava?"

"Safe and ready to see her shero."

"I'm not much of a shero, but I'm glad I could get her free from Cayum."

"He's a nasty and vicious piece of work. I'll give him that."

"You sound like that's a good thing."

"The Fae are ageless, living long beyond the human concept of time. I'd like to pretend we are all sunshine and roses, but we are far from that. Those of us who live without going mad learn to balance the dark and the light within ourselves.

"Dark and light only refer to our power source. Dark Fae pull power from the moon, the stars, and the very darkness itself. While light Fae worship the sun, and all that entails, they are no less viscous."

"Good to know."

"I'm sure you know more about Cayum than you want to."

"I know too much for his liking, but I'm not interested in turning him into the authorities. I don't want to kill for him anymore. Ava is safe, my contract is over."

"He won't see it that way."

"I know. I haven't figured out the next step yet. Just the first few. Get Ava to safety, win my ninth and final title, and get the hell out of dodge."

Synne disappeared into the walk-in closet, appearing a few minutes later with jeans, a long-sleeved t-shirt, and black leather boots. Laying them on the bed before rummaging around in a drawer.

"Cotton, silk, or lace? Thong or bikini?"

"Cotton and do you have boxers?

"I have a pair of Devil's. Don't worry, he goes commando I bought him a pair so I could wear them around the cabin."

"Are you two a thing?"

"We are enjoying each other's company, nothing serious."

"Good for you."

After all the clothes lay on the bed, Synne used magick to make them adjustable. In essence, the clothes would fit themselves to her body as she put them on. Synne continued to talk as she dressed.

"You'll have to ride on one of the brothers' bikes. I can't portal you."

"They're brothers? Yeah, I get it. Energy signature and all. I'm sure Cayum is tracking me as we speak."

"Yes, but there are enough wards here to buy us a few if not several hours. Even then it will take a lot to break the wards his best hope is to lure you out once he finds you. Our job will be to lure him in this direction and be long gone by the time he arrives. The boys belong to Odin's Wolves."

"I've heard that name before."

Chapter 7

Death

She dressed quickly, heading downstairs grateful for the smell of cooking meat, and the fates. How else would she be surrounded by the two people she was set to rendezvous with and his brother who happened to be her rescue cop? She'd heard of Odin's Wolves. A group of one hundred warriors infused with Odin's essence. Shifter warriors created by Gaia to be Earth's guardians. The first shifters.

Even living on the streets most of her life she'd heard the tales and stories of the wolves.

Something pricked at her consciousness, some memory that seemed buried deep, wanted to be free. The more time she spent around the cop, Logan, Viper, whatever his name was, the more the memory wanted to surface. She knew him, but from where?

"What's cooking and why do you call the cop Viper?"

Devil, who stood in front of the stove, a large griddle filled with breakfast meats, had what she would call a shit-eating grin turning up the corners of his mouth. Viper spit a sip of coffee all over the counter.

"Fuck! Don't say a fucking word."

"Already told you it would happen. His name's Viper because Anaconda takes too long to say."

It took her a few seconds to catch on; she wasn't stupid, but she didn't expect that. She should: after all, guys will be guys.

"As long as it's not because he's done in a flat second, it's all good."

Where the fuck did that come from? Maybe she retired as the shy, quiet girl with Lady Death.

"No worries there, sweet cheeks," Viper chuckled.

"Call me sweet cheeks again and I'll cut you."

Her deadpan response must have surprised him, he took a full thirty seconds before replying.

"Good to know. I like living on the edge."

"Question is, can you handle the heat?" *What the actual fuck is coming out of my mouth?*

"Maybe we should get you some food, Billie. Your energy was pretty low and now you have all our energy inside you. It might not be digested yet."

Her eyes widened. That explained it. Though she kinda liked the spunk. It felt so free to say what was on your mind. She had to guard every word around Cayum.

"How do you like your ribeye?"

"I did smell steak. Medium-rare please."

"Coming right up, along with eggs, hope you like scrambled."

"Scrambled is fine, thank you."

Devil loaded a plate and handed it to her. She sat down at the table, digging in with gusto. Billie felt better after she finished her second plate.

"How soon can we get on the road?"

"We can leave as soon as we finish cleaning up," Devil replied. "There's extra coats in the hall closet. One of them should fit you. You'll have to ride passenger with one of us."

"Not a problem, I'm ready to get on the road.

Viper

Less than an hour later they were on the road. Billie chose to ride behind him. Her long dark hair pulled into a braid with a bandana tied around it to help keep her head warm. Arms wrapped around him, she held on tight as they took the curves in the road in perfect synchronicity.

They decided to take the back roads in hopes it would keep Cayum off their trail longer. The more distance they put between them and the cabin the better off they'd be. Not that he was worried about fighting the Dark Fae or his minions if they had too. It wouldn't be the first time he'd dealt with Tromluí, just the first time dealing with this particular Dark Fae.

Less than twenty minutes away from the base, he knew their luck ran out. He could sense the other shifters waiting for them not far from where they were. Viper signaled to Devil to pull over.

"Company up ahead."

Devil grinned. "Let's get it."

"You feel powered up enough to fight?"

"I'm not at a hundred percent, but I'm ready and willing to fight."

They pulled the bikes off the road and into a copse of trees. Heading toward the ambush by foot he hoped to surprise their adversaries. On silent feet, they moved over the barren ground. Snow hadn't fallen in a few weeks, the ground not yet frozen solid had some give to it.

Less than a hundred yards away Viper spotted a motley group of paranormal creatures. Cayum must be serious about getting Billie back. Four shifters, half a dozen hobgoblins, and Cyclops, and a witch waited for them.

Viper motioned for them to turn around. He found a tight copse of evergreen trees a few hundred yards back. Pulling the jamming device out of his pocket he pressed the button enacting its power before he spoke.

"This should be far enough away they won't notice it. I doubt the witch is looking for a privacy device."

"That's Maeve, one Cayum's top witches. I'll take her out first, by that I mean render her unconscious as soon as possible. I don't want her to know I'm coming for her. So, I'll charge the Cyclops."

"Devil, can you take out the hobgoblins? I didn't take the time to see what kind of shifters he sent. I may need backup."

"A wolf, a tiger, and two bears."

"Yeah buddy, you keep them busy until I take out the hobgoblins."

"I'm going to go around and go in from the side in between Maeve and the Cyclops."

Viper knew she could handle herself; his focus was on the group of shifters. Devil would be coming in from a different direction in this three-pronged attack.

He paused on the edge of the clearing, waiting for Devil's signal.

"Yoo-hoo, boys, my bike broke down. I wondered if one of you big strong handsome men could come help little ol' me?"
Viper chuckled under his breath; leave it to Mr. Flamboyant. He counted to five stepping out as the hobgoblins took off after Devil the shifters laughing. The laugh was about to be on them. They had no idea they were in for a world of hurt.

"Something funny, douchebag?" he called out as he stepped into the clearing. Six heads turned his way. Billie would be doing her thing in less than sixty seconds if timing went right.

"Who are you calling a douchebag? the biggest one roared.

"You for sure. You're the ugliest motherfucker I've ever seen. I bet your mother had to put pork chops around your neck to get the dogs to play with you."

Douchebag one let out a roar like a bear and charged him without shifting. After he easily side-stepped the bear, his friends decided to join in.

Bear two began to shift, and rather clumsily at that. The tiger rushed him, shifting his fingers into claws. He had superior control over his animal. One to watch for. He took the razor claws across the arm, kicking at the tiger's kneecap, he heard a satisfying pop in time for bear two to finish shifting and head his way.

The wolf had taken time to circle around behind him taking time to change forms he headed toward him roughly opposite of the bear.

Viper stood his ground until the last second, channeling his wolf and leaping out of the way. The bear and wolf collided, teeth gnashing and claws ripping. It would take them a moment to get out of that.

Chapter 8

Death

She picked up a handful of loose dirt and gravel, holding it in one hand. Billie heard all hell break loose and knew it was her turn to act.

"Maeve, I see you brought your boyfriend. We should double date sometime."

"You're in a lot of trouble Billie. Just come peacefully and Cayum will go easier on you."

"Yeah, I don't think so. I'm not going back. My contract is finished and so am I."

"You'll wish you were finished after Cayum gets done with you."

Maeve motioned to the Cyclops, who headed in her direction at a sprint while she undoubtedly prepared a spell. Billie ran toward the Cyclops, picking up speed. If the beast thought she was playing chicken, he didn't blink. He started moving faster in her direction. Billie picked up more speed, needing to make the timing just right.

She launched her body toward the Cyclops when he stopped to react, she jumped, twisting to the side, and throwing the debris into it's one large eye. It grabbed its eye, screaming.

Billie continued on her trajectory, tackling Maeve. She ran her head into the ground, knocking her out. At least that's all Billie hoped she did, no tell-tale crack, hopefully, meant she didn't break her permanently. After all, the woman was doing her job. One that Cayum paid her well for.

A large hand wrapped around her ankle, pulling her off Maeve's prone form. The enraged Cyclops picked her up by her ankle and threw her across the clearing. She landed with a thud into a group of trees, knocking the breath out of her. This time she heard a crack, or three.

Billie managed to get up and out of the way of the charging Cyclops. The creature seemed enraged at what she'd done to Maeve, maybe it was hers. All she knew was she needed to stay out of the way and form a quick fighting tactic. This time, when the creature swung one meaty fist at her, she ducked, under-delivering three quick punishing blows to his side before dodging out of the way.

He swung around, screeching at her like a mad beast swinging wildly. Apparently, he was used to having the upper hand. Billie used his anger to her advantage. Using her superior reflexes to dodge out of the way, occasionally she'd get in a good jab to the ribs. The fourth time she connected, the force sent the Cyclops back five feet. She heard the crunch of bone.

Her mimic ability picked up the Cyclops' preternatural strength, which was greater than her own. The creature, beyond reason, uprooted a tree and started swinging it at her like a club. She managed to dodge most of it. A few branches slipped through her defenses a few times. Her body tingled with warm heat, her vision blurring for a split second. Just long enough for the Cyclops to land a decent blow with one of the tree's larger limbs to her head, splitting it open above her right eye. Blood poured from the wound, running into her eyes.

Billie closed her eyes, using her other senses rather than fighting impaired, to track the Cyclops by sound. She waited, unmoving, until the Cyclops was in reach. Rolling out of the way, she did a kip-up regaining her feet. Billie grabbed a pole sized branch not far away, hitting the Cyclops in the back of the head. His swing overbalanced him enough to give her the advantage.

Billie pressed the advantage. Kicking the creature's legs out from under it as it turned around.

Once on the ground, she drove the end of the stick into its eye socket with all her might. Her efforts met with a sickening squelch. She may not like killing, but she was good at it. Wanting to put the Cyclops out of its misery, she retrieved a wicked-looking knife from Maeve's side and plunged it through the Cyclops' rib cage and into his heart, killing him instantly.

Viper

He didn't have time to see how either of his companions fared. His hands were full with two large bears and a wolf. One bear uninjured, and the tiger would be back on his feet soon. Viper needed to take one of these guys out and fast. He shifted as he moved into combat-form. Over twelve feet tall with thick black fur, razor teeth, and claws. Not to mention superior strength and agility skills in this form.

He threw back his head and howled, before throwing himself at bear one. The bear moved too slow; Viper clamped his teeth on the fleshy underpart of the bear's throat, ripping it out.

Blood squirted everywhere; he heard the other bear's roar and knew it was time to move. While he'd have liked to finish the kill, he didn't have that luxury. Three other opponents surrounded him, and now they had no reason to hold back. Not that he thought they were going to. Billie was the only one they needed alive.

He heard Devil's howl and knew backup was on the way. Bear two changed into his combat-form, matching Viper for height but outweighing him by a couple of hundred pounds. The bear's claws, like six-inch daggers, swiped at him. He managed to dodge out of the way. Taking the wolf by surprise, he used the wolf's body to put distance between him and the bear.

Sharp pain in his calf told him he hadn't managed to avoid the tiger. Pain ripped through his leg as the tiger's jaws clamped down. *Fuck!* He used one fist like a hammer to smash the tiger in the top of the head, luckily Devil came into the clearing garnering the attention of bear two.

Viper smashed the tiger in the head twice more; the last time he heard a loud crack. His speed was faster than most wolves; he managed to kill the tiger before the wolves' claws ripped into his back.

With the tiger's jaws still locked around his leg, he dodged the next few lunges from the wolf. Knowing he only had one shot at this he grabbed a hold of the wolf as he lunged wrestling him to the ground in a bear hug. Viper managed to use his superior strength to squeeze the wolf until he lost consciousness. Dropping the wolf to the ground, he forced the tiger's jaws from around his leg, managing to get untangled by the time Devil finished the bear. He turned in time to see Billie plunge a knife into the Cyclops' heart.

Viper walked over to make sure bear one was dead; he didn't want the shifter suffering.

"I'll call for a cleanup. Who's alive?
"The witch and the wolf?"

Chapter 9

Viper

Viper, Billie, and Devil hopped back on their bikes, making it the rest of the way to White Horse safely. Devil led the way through the small town to an old schoolhouse no longer in use. He drove around behind the building before bringing his custom bike to a halt.

"I'll take you to the sleeping quarters." Viper said to Billie as they climbed off the bikes.

The blood in his veins was still filled with adrenaline after the fight with the shifters. Billie's body heat as she held on tight nearly had him over the edge. He reached for Billie's hand. She looked down at it as her brows furrowed.

"I'm not gonna bite you unless you like that sort of thing," he said with a smirk and a wink.

Billie smiled back and took his hand, following him through the metal door. The door opened into a long hallway. Two sets of double doors led to the gymnasium on the left side. He peeked into the right door on the right side, it was set up as a common room. Couches, recliners, big screen TV, refrigerator, microwave, and a sink.

They continued down the hall. Devil said to turn right at the end of the hall, then another right. The classrooms started here and were being slowly converted into bedroom suites. Devil said each would have a full bath, a kitchenette, small dining/sitting area. Mother wanted the entire building set up with the fastest internet magick could produce.

Viper chose the second door on the right. He led Billie through the door into a room and closed the door. He stepped up to her, his eyes roaming all over her body. "I saw you kill that Cyclops. You're so fucking bad-ass Billie. Are you injured?"

She shook her head. Her scent was driving him insane. He couldn't help himself as he reached up and touched her cheek.

Billie stepped back from his touch. "What are you doing?"

He stepped closer. "I can't help it. There's this energy I feel when I'm near you. I want to protect you, keep you safe. With me."

He leaned in and kissed her softly. Billie leaned in, returning the kiss with a moan. He gripped her hips, pulling her closer as she wrapped her arms around his broad shoulders.

Viper's tongue slid into her mouth. Her hardened nipples pressed up against his chest. His massive dick was hard as he scooped her up into his arms and carried her to the bed.

He laid her on the bed and covered her body with his, nestling his hips in between her supple thighs. There was a look of fear in Billie's eyes for a quick moment. Viper nuzzled her neck. "I'll go slow, Billie. We're alone and there's no need to rush this okay?"

"Sure," she replied, pulling him down to kiss him again. But the way she kissed him said the complete opposite as their tongues clashed, wrestling in a heated frenzy.

Viper's hips ground against her pelvis and he watched her eyes go wide.

"Oh my. Will it even fit?"

Viper smirked, brushing his fingertips across her cheek. "I guarantee it will."

He smothered her with kisses again, then slid his tongue along her soft neck, biting and nibbling.

Billie gripped his broad shoulders, digging her nails into his skin. He could smell her arousal. Viper sat up and pulled his shirt off. "It'd much easier if we stripped out of these clothes."

Within seconds, both were naked, and with one swift move, Billie straddled her thighs over Viper's hips.

"Well okay then!" Viper said, as his hands went to her supple and strong thighs. *Her skin is so soft.*

Death

Billie slid the head of Viper's cock along her tight opening, and a shiver of excitement ran through her. Viper pulled her down and kissed her, his tongue darting out, then pushing through her lips.

She moaned, tangling her tongue with his, and slowly lowered herself on his thick cock. Her opening was tight but slick with wetness and Viper raised his hips to meet hers. For a fleeting moment, she worried that she would only feel pain. But Viper was gentle and patient, kissing her while his warm hands caressed her thighs and hips. She lowered herself even more and was stretched and fully impaled on him.

"You're so tight and feel so damn good Billie," Viper groaned.

Billie moaned, riding him. She picked up the pace, sliding up and down his hard shaft. Viper's hand glided along her inner thigh and reached her sensitive spot. He rubbed Billie there with his thumb, and she breathed heavy and fast until she cried out her release in an exploding orgasm.

Viper

"Did that feel good baby?"
"Yes."

"I'm going to make you feel even better. He flipped them so she was on her back and began kissing down her neck to her breasts, nipping hard enough to leave little marks along her skin. She gasped as his teeth dug into the soft flesh of her under breast. Viper applied enough pressure to incite the pleasure/pain principle.

His hot tongue lathed the nipples of each breast until they were stiff peaks. Billie moaned and writhed under his erotic ministrations. He slid down farther, burying his face into her wetness.

"Damn, baby you taste good."

Her only reply was another moan as his tongue flicked the swollen bundle of nerves in between her legs. Her hips bucked off the bed as she cried out in ecstasy.

"Turn over for me."

Billie turned over onto her stomach.

"Now get on your hands and knees."

She got on her hands and knees. Her ass up high in the air legs spread wide. Viper paused to admire the beauty in front of him. Damn, he could get used to this. He got behind her, positioning the head of his cock at her slick entrance.

He drove into the hilt on the first thrust. Her hips bucked to meet his. Viper drove into her relentlessly, all the while one his fingers traced the feather tattoo on her back. Perhaps the most intricate tattoo he'd ever seen.

"You're so fucking hot."

"Shut up and fuck me harder."

He chuckled, increasing his speed. Thrusting fast and deep, her cries became louder. Juices ran down both of their legs. She began to clench and release her inner muscles, the motions milking his cock.

"Fuck, baby. I'm going to come."

Viper came with a roar spilling his seed deep inside her. He pulled out, gathering her in his arms.

Chapter 10

Viper

He left Billie to sleep soundlessly in the room they shared. Synne waited for him by the back entrance, which was currently the main entrance to the sleeping rooms/soon to be housing quarters. She looked off toward the edge of the woods several hundred yards away.

"Cayum will be here soon. He'll challenge you and demand retribution for interfering with his property."

"Can we buy out her contract?"
Synne looked at him for a long moment before answering, "How deep are your pockets?"

"I have some cash and things I can liquidate. If we need fast cash the brothers will pitch in."

"Are you all secret millionaires?"

"We've been around a long time; it would be irresponsible not to put away for the future."

Her blue eyes glowed with powerful energy as she "looked" at him. Sizing up his preternatural abilities.

"You'd give Cayum a run for his money, probably beat him, but he doesn't fight fair, and he never fights alone. If you can broker a deal, you best get it done before Lady Death awakens from her slumber."

"What did you do?"

"Bought you time. It's not my story to tell, but her scars run deeper than the one on her side."

"Cayum did that, didn't he?"

"Yes."

Viper fought the urge to go ballistic and rip the motherfucker's head off his shoulders at first sight. He didn't want to start a war with the Tromluí, not unless there was no other way to protect what was his.

He rolled that word around in his mind since he couldn't remember the last time he thought of a woman as his. Not property. His to love, respect, and protect. His to nurture and show a side that no one else got to see. He swallowed the thought both terrified and intrigued him.

"One day I will take my vengeance upon him. I swear by Odin, he will pay for marking what is mine."

Mate, his wolf whispered. He didn't feel the mating bond. Should he?

"I need to talk to Omen."

"You need a seer?"

"Yes, something isn't right."

"First, I acknowledge and grant you a boon when it's time. Second, remember for that wound, killing an immortal is not considered equal vengeance."

"Equal vengeance. You measure them?"

"Yes, the Fae world is not like this one. We work in the old ways. An eye for an eye is still literal in many ways. You can bargain for the eye if you don't want to lose yours."

"So, what if I want to kill the motherfucker, I have to barter with him?"

"No, you barter with the court. Since he's a minor member and a Capo, you'd have to bargain to kill him without retribution from one or both sides."

"That's way too much political bullshit for me."

She smiled, "Welcome to my world."

"I'll pass, but I'd appreciate your counsel through this. How do I hire you?"

Synne laughed, "You can hire me the old-fashioned way, with money. Lots of it. Unless you have an antiquity, I might want. You mentioned liquidating some assets."

It was his turn to laugh. "At least you're upfront."

"Any time I can be. Politics wears on my nerves. It's why I only go to court when his royal high*nass* commands me too."

"That bad?"

"Yes. I'll see if I can find a seer for you. I know one or two, I need to check their whereabouts. You might have to travel."

"I can do that. Thank you."

"Hey, I'm on retainer now as your Fae liaison. I'll send you a bill, with the friends and family discount. Keep that in mind if you refer me. I'm expensive as fuck and worth every cent. Now, you need to go gather your brothers. You can bring five with you, per Cayum's parle reply. Bring seven. He always lies about the number of people he's bringing.

"If you have a mage or witch, bring them as well. He won't rely on muscle alone."

"How much time do I have?"

"Three hours and fifteen minutes. You must meet in the center of the woods. It's roughly two and a half miles southeast of here."

"How long will she sleep?"

"I'm not sure, exactly. She has incredible regenerative abilities, but whatever she did to survive that crash and evade Cayum's first attempt at retrieving her depleted all her energy down to the cellular level. I added a sleeping spell to that to make sure she stays under until tomorrow early afternoon. We need time to take care of this, and her body needs to heal. I'll take the flack."

"Thanks, but not necessary. If she's mad, she can be mad at me. I don't think she's going to like me going to Cayum behind her back."

"Not behind her back, you're going to represent her, while she's somewhere safe."

"I don't think she'll see it that way. You said her scars run deep. I've spent too much time on the battlefield not to realize when someone is shell shocked. When they've seen more than their brain can handle. They shove it so far into the back of their mind, it may never see the light of day.

"But the energy to keep it buried weighs heavily on you. It haunts you. I looked into her eyes earlier, she's haunted."

"Likely from the things she's done for him."

"That's part of it, I have no doubt, but there is more. I don't know. It's part of why I want to meet with a seer."

"Good to know. I'll take that into consideration when I make queries."

"I'll see you in a few hours and thank you."

"Don't forget, presentation counts when it comes to the Fae. Dress well."

"Are you fucking kidding me?"

"Not even a little bit. This is a display of power and wealth."

"It's a goddamned pissing contest."

"Exactly, wolf. If you want that woman you marked, you best be on point."

"Fuck me!"

"Maybe later, I'm currently enthralled by your brother."

Unsure how to respond to that, he simply turned on his heel and headed to find Blade.

He found Devil before he found Blade.

"I need your help."

"What do you need?"

Viper gave him a brief rundown of his conversation with Synne. "That's a tall order. Elvis is here. I'll get him to put together the wardrobe. Mother will pitch in too, I'm sure. He's always up on the latest Fae Fashion?"

"Really?"

"It will take him what, sixty seconds, to find out on the internet?"

"True. Thank Odin for our techno mage. Something I know Cayum won't have. I think we should bring Beast as well. Paradox twins are rare and being together at the same location at the same time, rarer still.

"You, me, Beast, Blade, Elvis, and Mother. We need one more."

"Two. I don't count. Cayum will bring seven. I have an idea. You get everything ready. I'll be back in two and a half hours."

Viper headed to his bike hoping he could find Nic in time. He met the Amir several years ago when a rogue vampire turned serial killer left bodies all over the city. An Amir is basically a prince or leader of an area. In this case, he ran Dallas, Oklahoma City, Tulsa, and the surrounding area.

He worked with Nic to track down and exterminate the rogue vampire. The final showdown happened about forty-five minutes from there in an old Gothic estate. Nic said he planned on taking the property over and making it his new headquarters.

He made the ride in thirty minutes. Two miles before the entrance, an eight-foot-tall wrought iron fence topped with spear tips appeared along the property. Massive wrought iron gates blocked the entrance. Viper pushed the intercom button, after waiting for a reply he tried one more time.

When no one replied he parked his bike; shifting in combat form he easily leaped over the fence. As soon as he topped the fence, he felt energy rush over him. The property must be warded. He most likely broke the ward and alerted someone of his arrival.

During the day, most of Nic's companions would be sleeping in light-proof rooms. Nic entertained a variety of paranormals, so anyone could be there. He didn't worry about it. Shifting into a massive wolf, he ran the distance between the gate and the house.

When he didn't encounter anyone, he shifted back to human form, knocking on the door.

Chapter 11

Viper

A swarthy, dark-haired man answered the door. Viper didn't recognize him, so he must be new in Nic's employ.

"How may I help you?"

"Name's Logan Haagan. I'm here to see Nic on an urgent matter."

"Master Nic is normally unavailable at his hour, can it not wait until after sundown?"

"I'm afraid I don't have time."
The man opened the door. "Please come in."

Viper followed him through the door and down the hall into a large room.

"If you will wait here, I will fetch Master Nic."

He stood in the parlor of the home. It very much reminded him of a Gothic Victorian he once owned in Philadelphia during the 1800s. The parlor was decorated in silver and blue, no doubt for the new year. If memory served him correctly, Nic liked to host parties and made sure whatever home he lived in at the time was not only immaculate but ready for him to invite guests over at a whim.

The man that answered the door returned to the room with a silver tray, a decanter of cognac, two glasses, and what looked to be a cigar box.

"Mr. Haagan, please have a seat and allow me to pour you a drink. My name is Ander Ciric. Please call me Ander. I'm here to assist you in any way possible."

"Thank you, Ander. Is that a humidor?

"Yes, sir. Would you like one? Hand-rolled Cubans."

"I would."

Ander allowed him to select a cigar before snipping off one end and handing it back to him, lighter held at the ready. Hmm, he wondered if Omen would let them hire a butler for the clubhouse. Only members and their family would be in the housing quarters.

He enjoyed the cigar, taking a long pull, savoring the flavor before he took a sip of the cognac. Delicious.

"Hello, my friend, it's good to see you."

Viper didn't hear him enter; he didn't need to. The vampire's power preceded him down the hall.

"How is your cognac?"

He put down the cigar and drink, offering his hand to Nic in a firm shake.

"Amazing hospitality as always."

Nic sat in the chair across from his, Anders poured him a drink before preparing a cigar and handing it to his master.

"Thank you, Anders. I'll call if I need you."

Anders bowed before backing out of the room and closing the doors behind him.

"To what do I owe the honor of your visit?"

"Always the polite one."

Nic smiled, showing perfect white teeth. "Much like you I come from an earlier time. One where people had manners. It's not like you take advantage of our acquaintance, Viking."

"I'll do my best not to do that, yet I did come to ask a favor. A boon to be bargained for now or named another time."

Nic whistled with a gleam in his eyes a split second. "A boon from one of Odin's own to a vampire to be named later. This must be a large favor indeed."

"It involves the Tromluí. I need the power to bargain. In short, I need you and someone else to bring to the table."

He glanced at his watch. "In about ninety-minutes, I have to meet Cayum, a Tromluí capo, to bargain for a woman's life."

"What does this woman mean to you?"

"Honestly, I don't know. I have a gut feeling that it's something important. Something I should remember."

"Let me catch your eyes, wolf?"

"What? Why?"

Nic, instead of being insulted, laughed. "First, I may be old, but I'm not sure even I could roll a godling's mind. With your permission, allowance, I want to see if someone has messed with your memories."

"I thought only mesmers could do that?"

"Mesmers, and a few others. It's a gift of mine, I don't use it often, nor do I allow others to know I have the ability. I'm trusting you as much as you will need to trust me. The sword cuts both ways."

"I taste the truth of your words."

"Just relax and fall into my gaze."

"Said the spider to the fly."

He heard Nic chuckle. "Good thing for you, I do not take offense easily."

"I wouldn't say it If I thought you'd actually be offended."

"Good point. Shall we begin?"

"Yeah, sorry."

Viper drew a few deep breaths to steady his nerves; giving a vampire a path into his mind could spell disaster on many levels. Vampires could control another being once they were deep enough inside your mind. Sleepers had zero chance of resisting a vampire as powerful as Nic. He could roll their mind in under ten seconds. It would take him longer to roll or take over another preternatural being's mind, but he'd seen it happen. Not many beings were impervious to the gaze of a vampire: the more powerful the vampire, the stronger their gaze.

He relaxed, looking directly into Nic's blue eyes. The color intensified glowing slightly before his pupils began to bleed out and eat up all the color. A fathomless field of darkness greeted him as the vampire's gaze penetrated the barriers of his mind and began to explore its deep recesses.

Viper had no idea how long he was lost in Nic's gaze only that the vampire withdrew, and his mind was his own once again.

"There is a block there of a sort."

"Can you expound on that?"

Nic shook his head. "Not much. The memory has not been taken or changed. Something is simply blocking you from remembering it."

"You can't tell what?"

"No, If I took a guess, I'd say magick, but not a mesmer's magick. Not Fae magick either."

"Well, fuck."

"Precisely. Now about your other query. I'll take the favor owed. I think we trust each other enough. Yes?"

"Agreed. Before we make this pact official, I need to finish things up on my end. Do you have anyone else you can bring?"

"Who are we meeting again?"

"Fae's name is Cayum."

"Oh yes, I know that one. We've done business a time or two. I do know someone, but I warn you my price will have to be steep to make this a fair trade."

"If it turns the tables on Cayum and saves Billie and Ava. I'm willing to do it."

"Ava, is she a pookah, by chance?

"Yes."

"I have just the right person to bring. I'll have to meet you there. "No worries. Give me general directions."

"It's not going to be full dark."

"Not a problem for either of us."

Viper drew a vicious looking dagger from its sheath in his belt. He sliced his palm before handing the dagger to Nic. Nic licked the blood off the dagger before slicing his palm.

"Waste not, and all that," Nic said offering his freshly cut hand.

"In exchange for your help with Cayum, I owe you one boon to be named at a later date."

"Agreed."

When their hands clasped together, their blood mingled, shooting energy up his arm as the magick behind the boon took hold. If he judged Nic wrong he could be in a world of hurt, yet he somehow instinctively knew saving Billie would be worth so much more to him.

Chapter 12

Viper

Synne met them at the edge of the woods. She wore an elaborate black and red dress, the style dating back a few hundred years, much like the armor he and his brothers wore. The dress was adorned with real golden thread and dozens of deep ruby red gems. Her black hair was braided with large diamonds down the length of it. A priestess woad glowed golden in the center of her forehead. A half dozen golden hoops decorated with diamonds graced each of her pointed ears.

"They're already gathered, let me take a look at you."

Synne gave them each an appraising look. Elvis had chosen their outfit. Dark metal with intricate scrollwork and gold trim, with a large valknut in the center of their chest. The heavily detailed armor had been magically reinforced to take an extreme amount of damage. His ornate helm with horns tucked under one arm, his red cape blowing with the wind. He and his brothers cut quite a figure in their official uniforms. In the armor, he and Beast looked identical. Elvis, Mother, Blade, and Devil stood beside him.

"Cayum is already here, as predicted he brought two others.

"Our other two will be here shortly. Let's begin the procession."

"You want to begin without a full showing?"

"Yes."

"Hmm, you must have something up your sleeve."

"Indeed."

They gathered information, Viper in the lead. Blade at his right elbow, Beast at his left. Powerful energy washed over them as they stepped from the mortal world through the portal and into a sacred space. The world had several such hidden places of power. Each one was considered sacred ground. Blood spilled on sacred ground was an offense and punishable by everlasting torture.

The last man to test the sacred space and had been strapped to the side of a mountain. Every morning a Keeper would slice open the man's guts to let birds and other animals feast on him while he still lived. He would be restored whole each night to wait in darkness for the next morning. Viper shuddered at the thought of enduring that torture for eternity.

The portal led them to a deep underground cavern. Glowing moss lit the room in soft blue light. A large magical orb hung in mid-air like a moon glowing in the inky blackness of the cavern's roof. He couldn't tell how far up the ceiling was. Hard to judge with magickal places. A circle formed as they approached the center, creating magick that was needed for the meeting automatically.

Cayum appeared on the opposite side of the cavern. Two redcaps, each with a barghest, accompanied him, two Dark Faes stood on either side, and the last to the party, an obsidian witch.

Redcaps rarely left Faerie unless it involved battle, and they loved spilling blood. Barghest were demon dogs that devoured everything in sight, though they could be trained to restrain themselves. He'd had one for a century or so. He had no idea who the Dark Faes were, either bodyguards or other Tromluí. The obsidian witch would have been Cayum's ace in the hole. Obsidian witches were feared by most and for good reason. They were formidable foes that few survived.

Synne walked to the center of the cavern floor. A softly glowing dais formed beneath her elevating her up four feet from the floor.

"We are ready, Shadow Princess," Cayum called out before she asked. He seemed to be in a hurry to get things started.

"Thank you, Cayum. Third son of Kallum, Capo of the Tromluí." She turned her attention to him. "Viper, Logan Haagan, son of Odin & Gaia, member of the hundred, are you ready?"

Viper stepped forward bowing his head. "We ask...."

Before he got any further, a cold wind blew across the cavern. Fat flakes of snow fell from the false sky, dusting the floor. An orb of white light descended from where the "moon" hung in the sky. The orb grew larger as it descended. Once it reached the floor a few feet from Viper the light began to recede, revealing Nic and a Fae he didn't recognize.

Her pale skin looked like soft moonlight, her lips like two ripe berries, with silver eyes that looked in his direction. She wore a silver, white, and blue dress covered in expensive jewels. A vine of ice crawled up one arm. Flowers made of ice bloomed in front of his eyes before closing and blooming again. A crown of ice and snow graced her silver-white hair. Hair she'd been born with and not gotten from age if he had to guess. Enormous, delicate blueish white wings fluttered behind her, snow falling with every move.

Nic bowed to Synne, a charming smile on his face, he made sure to flash fang so there would be no doubt what he was. Viper had seen Nic do it before.

"Princess of Shadows, may I introduce her royal highness Leandra, Queen of the Winter court."

Synne and everyone else in the room bowed. "Your Majesty. Which side are you here to represent?"

Her voice, though soft, carried an enormous amount of power, it whispered across his skin when she spoke. His bones ached from being so close to ancient power.

"I'm here on behalf of Odin and his wolves."

He heard Cayum say a string of curse words. The balance of power had clearly swung in their direction. Nic said he would owe him big time; the vampire was true to his word.

"Now that all parties have arrived, we can begin the negotiations. By the power vested to me by Danu, our great mother, I call us to order. Cayum, since you are the aggrieved, you may state your case first.

Cayum came forward, stepping to the right of Synne, another dais appeared raising him a few feet off the floor.

"I am here to claim retribution on Billie Cameron, who not only broke her contract, but also stole my property. I demand their return or compensation equal to their value."

"Is Billie Cameron here to answer the charges?" Synne paused allowing time for the silence to answer. "Who here represents Miss Cameron?"

Viper stepped forward, "I represent Miss Cameron and her ward, the pookah, Ava. We are here to negotiate compensation for the contract of Billie Cameron and the ownership of the pookah, Ava."

Viper was relieved Billie wasn't here to witness this, certain that she'd have an aversion to them buying Ava. Ownership of the girl through Cayum would keep her safe, no matter what they had to do.

"Cayum, present Billie Cameron's contract along with Ava's ownership papers."

Cayum nodded to the Dark Fae on his left, and he pulled the papers out of his pocket, offering them to Synne. She reached down; the papers floated from his hand up to hers.

Synne drew a rune of power over the papers. The rune glowed red before setting the papers on fire and engulfing them in flames.

"Cayum, you may begin opening terms."

"One hundred million dollars for each contract plus one of the wolves must become my servant for the term of three years."

Viper's temper flared. He never wanted to rip someone's head off as much as he did Cayum's at this very moment. He intended to state his grievance after the negotiations were finished. Politics were the bane of his existence, one of the reasons he stayed out of the top ranks of the wolves. He had plenty of leadership ability but lacked the desire to play the politics needed to lead ninety-nine other alpha wolf shifters.

"Viper, your reply."

He clenched his jaw, balling his free hand into a fist. "Third term flat refused. Billie's contract was officially fulfilled by the win of her ninth title, no compensation is offered at this time for a completed contract. We offer ten million for the pookah, Ava."

"You'll pay for that offense wolf."

"Watch your tongue, son of Kallum, lower noble of the court. You're on sacred ground in the middle of a negotiation. One which the balance of power is not in your favor."

"My apologies, Princess of Shadows. Billie Cameron did not carry out the final kill, therefore she did not complete her contract. Seventy-five million for the pookah, Ava, and a wolf will owe me a boon."

"Your response?" Synne added.

"Query. Did the contract state Miss Cameron had to kill her final opponent?"

"Let me review the contract."

The paper returned from ashes to whole in the form of a scroll. She unrolled it before going over it thoroughly.

"There is no mention in the contract of Miss Cameron's requirement to kill her opponent."

"That part of the contract was verbal."

Viper could smell the lie from across the room, only he knew it wouldn't matter.

"Do you have a witness?"

The obsidian witch stepped forward raising her hand.

Synne turned to him, "Do you have a witness to dispute this?"

"I do not."

"Then the contract will be part of the negotiation. That brings it back to you, Viper."

"We offer five million for the contract, short one kill. Twenty-five million for the pookah, Ava, and a wolf will assist you once."

"I'm growing tired of your insults, wolf."

Viper's face remained impassive. Cayum didn't appreciate his low ball offers. Well, he didn't appreciate dealing with a scumbag.

"One hundred million for both contracts and one month of service from a wolf."

Finally, they were getting closer to a deal.

"Fifty million for both contracts and one-week bodyguard duty. The wolf does nothing against his principles."

"Seventy-five million, two weeks, and I choose the wolf."

"Seventy-five million, two weeks, it must be a wolf that is present. Nothing against his principles or will."

Leandra came forward. "Cayum, I require an oath. The wolf's will must be free at all times and required to do nothing against their principles."

Cayum stared at the Fae queen for a full two minutes before he replied.

"I swear to uphold the oath upon my word. If I should break the oath, my punishment is death."

"Which wolf do you choose?", Synne asked Cayum.

Cayum pointed to Elvis. "Him."

"Brother, is this acceptable?" Viper inquired.

"I accept under the oath given. When do I start my week?"

"I'd like to name the date later. Sometime within the next year. I need to consult my calendar."

"Agreed."

"Are all parties agreed to the terms?"

"Aye," said in near unison.

"I'll hold the papers until the funds have been delivered into Cayum's account. You have seventy-two hours to complete the exchange."

"Agreed."

"Blood must be offered to complete the deal."

Viper pulled the blade from its sheath, slicing his hand open he allowed the blood to drop to the ground.

Cayum pulled a slender silver dagger seemingly from thin air, slicing his palm before allowing the blood to fall to the ground. A burst of energy flooded the room with enough power to make his blood hum, culminating in a bright flash as the magick of the place cemented the deal.

"One last thing before we go. I claim the right of retribution against Cayum for the scar on Billie." He smiled, showing elongated teeth. "She's mine now."

"I'll report your claim to the courts," Synne said.

Chapter 13

Death

She dreamed of her time on the streets. A small child hiding from everything and everyone. It seemed everyone wanted a piece of her, even as a small child. Billie stayed on the streets until she met Cayum, never trusting anyone enough to let them take her. No, she tried that a few times. Each time ended in disaster with her life or virginity on the line.

Who the hell tries to sleep with a five-year-old? She didn't even know what the man was trying to do, only that she instinctively knew it was wrong. Billie told him to stop, she pushed him away, she even tried to hide. He kept coming after her. In the end, her powers kicked in and she didn't remember what happened. Only that when her memory came back, she stood in a puddle of his blood.

Cayum somehow found out about that murder and a few others. All done when she blacked out. All to save her life. She stopped blacking out at the age of thirteen. Each time after that, when it was her life or theirs, she remembered the killings. They made her feel dirty, somehow. None of them were done by choice. She hadn't set out to kill any of them, none of them gave her a chance.

The killings for Cayum were worse, each one cost her a little slice of her soul. Her only solace, each opponent that stepped in the ring knew there was a chance of death. Every time she won; more opponents would step up. They all wanted to test their mettle against the "little girl".

Billie topped six feet by her fourteenth birthday. She didn't have as many attackers by then. Cowards liked to prey on the small and weak. Something she vowed never to do. When she found Ava, Billie had no idea Cayum would take the girl, then use her as a bargaining tool. Billie only wanted to get the toddler to safety.

She found Ava alone, wandering the streets in a diaper at three in the morning in Kyoto, Japan. Needing to wind down after her latest fight, plus she always wanted to spend time in Japan. Cayum rarely gave her time off from the ring, not without threats and abuse.

When she tried to locate the girl's parents, she discovered that Ava's parents were killed. She found their bodies in a park, their throats slit, bodies drained of blood. A hunter must have found them, or they were sellers of pookah blood on the black market. Fae blood contained a great deal of magick, and it was highly prized and costly.

Knowing the child wouldn't be safe in foster care, she took her in. Billie kept her hidden for several days until she started crying uncontrollably when Billie was in the ring. One of Cayum's cronies found her, and the rest as they say is history.

Sitting up slowly, she looked around the room trying to get her bearings. She was in the clubhouse in White Horse.

Her stomach rumbling with hunger sent her in search of clothes to put on before she went looking for food. Billie's metabolism burned fast, she often consumed six meals a day to keep her body running.

Since she lost all her clothes in the accident, she rummaged around the drawers in the room she slept in. Finding a pair of sweats and t-shirt which she quickly pulled on, along with the boots Synne gave her earlier. She would need to go shopping for clothes.

Logan, err Viper, might take her, at the very least he'd point her in the right direction. A smile curved her lips thinking of him. Her lower body was still sore from their earlier activity. Damn, the man carried a tree trunk between his legs!

Billie wandered the halls, noting the layout to easily find her way back later. Following her nose, she smelled greasy, cheesy pizza.

Her stomach rumbled in anticipation. She entered a room that looked like an old cafeteria with a dozen or more mismatched tables and dozens of chairs. A large man with a shaved head carried a dozen or more pizza boxes in his hands, followed by Devil, who carried near the same amount.

"Hey, Lady D. You're just in time for pizza."

She grimaced. She hated that moniker.

"Can you call me Billie or Death."

"Sure can. Plates are through those doors. Do you mind grabbing a stack?"

"Not at all."

She hurried through the double doors grabbing a sleeve of paper plates, the only kind she found in the kitchen. By the time she carried them back out she spotted Ava and Logan, his brothers could call him Viper, walking hand in hand into the cafeteria.

Ava spotted her releasing Logan's hand; she ran toward Billie. Billie laughed. "Heads up."

As he looked up, she tossed him the sealed pack of plates before hurrying toward the little girl who wormed her way into the deepest part of Billie's heart. She caught Ava up in a hug, picking the girl up off her feet and swinging her around. Her heart felt lighter than, well, then she could remember in a long time.

"You were asleep for days, Billie. I got scared, but Logan told me you needed your sleep and would be fine."

"I must have been tired. Thank you for letting me sleep."

Her body must have gone into magickal hibernation mode after all.

"You're welcome. I want pizza."

Billie's stomach chose that time to rumble loudly, again. "Me too," she laughed.

"Logan got me cheese, extra-extra cheese, and mushrooms. I'll share it."

"You're not going to eat the whole pizza yourself?"

Ava's eyes widened. "It's a really big pizza, plus I had half a dozen burgers for lunch."

"We'll share then."

Billie rifled through the boxes until she found Ava's special pizza. She brought the large box over to the table, serving Ava a few slices before putting one on her plate. Logan sat another plate in front of her, piled high with various kinds of pizza.

"I didn't know what you liked, so I got you a variety."

"Thanks, I like everything but pineapple."

"I'm with you on that. Pineapple on pizza is an abomination."

"Agreed."

"Dig in, I'll go grab us a couple of beers."

"You don't have to do that. I can get my own."

"I know that but when did you last spend time with Ava?"

"It's been too long; months."

"Then I got this. You can grab me one another time."

"I want a red pop."

"I'll bring you one, and some extra napkins. Your face is saucy."

Billie watched Logan pick up a napkin and wipe pizza sauce off the pookah's face. Her heart warmed a touch more with every action he made since he picked her up off the roadside.

"Tell me what you have been up to while I've been sleeping."

"Oh, I've been playing. Most of this place is empty, plus there are dozens of hiding spots." Ava laughed mischievously. "Synne took me shopping to get clothes. She put a charm on us so no one would know we're different."

Billie shook her head. "One day, maybe we can walk the streets without hiding who we are."

Ava shook her head. "One day. Will you take me for ice cream and let everyone see my bunny ears?"

"If that's what you want."

"Oh, I do, and my pink hair. No one has pink hair. Well P!nk, but that's it mostly."

Billie laughed. "How about this Halloween you go as the real you?"

"What will you dress up as?"

"I don't know. Hmm. What if I went as Catwoman? You like her."

"Yes, but pink to match my hair."

"You want me to walk around in a pink leather catsuit?"

"Do I get a vote? I vote yes," Logan said, sitting a bottle of red pop in front of Ava before handing her a cold longneck bottle.

"But pink."

Ava, lost in a fit of giggles, didn't see the way Logan looked at her. She wondered if he was picturing her in the outfit or taking her out of it. Suddenly a form-fitting pink catsuit didn't seem so bad after all.

They each ate several slices of pizza, keeping the conversation light. If this kept up, Billie might actually feel happiness, real happiness. Something she never felt before, not in a long time anyway.

Someone or something was always there to rip it away from her. After Logan polished off his dozenth slice, she broached the subject of shopping.

"I need to get some clothes. Is there a car I can borrow?"

"I can take you if you want. I pulled some strings and got your ID replaced. I have no idea where you bank, so I couldn't get your card replaced."

"I hadn't thought about that. There should be funds in the local bank."

"I'll drive one of the cages and take you into town to get funds. Then head to Tulsa or Oklahoma City."

"Is that safe? Cayum is still out there. OMG. I can't believe I didn't think to ask. What happened, has he been here? Did he threaten anyone?"

"Synne helped us broker a deal."

"What kind of deal?"

"We gave him money, a lot of it."

"I'll pay you back every penny. I have a lot of money saved up. I'll give it to you as a down payment."

"Plenty of time to talk about that. There's no rush."

"Why are you being so nice?"

"Honestly?"

"Yes." She held her breath waiting for the answer.

"I like you, and I wanted to help, so I did."

"I don't want to owe anyone. Not after Cayum."

He put his hand on her shoulder leaning closer to her, "I understand. You need to get settled. We can talk about money in a few days."

"Ava do you want to go shopping?"

"No, Mother and I are playing video games. He even has some that haven't been released to the public yet."

Billie didn't remember meeting Mother; he must be one of the wolves. A heavily tattooed man with dark hair, dark eyes, and an infectious smile stood a few feet from Ava.

"Are you ready to go play that first shooter?"

"You know it!"

Billie watched them walk away. The smile on Ava's face told her whatever she'd have to pay would be worth it. The young pookah no longer had to worry about being sold into slavery or who knows what other sinister plan Cayum had for her.

"Mother will take good care of her. The kid's a gaming genius."

"Really? Cayum didn't allow us to spend much time together. Not once after he took her from me."

"Want to talk about it?"

"No, not really. How soon can we go?"

"I'm ready whenever you are."

Chapter 14

Death

It turns out that bikers referred to regular vehicles as a cage. They preferred the freedom of the open road. Viper climbed into the truck wearing a long-sleeved Henley shirt but not his cut. Bikers didn't wear them in cages.

"Maybe I should have raided your closet?"

He laughed, "Why's that?"

"Henley's are soft."

"Mmhmm, you can have one if you want."

His voice dropped a few octaves, the suggestive timber sent a tingle right between her thighs. Fuck! She didn't even have panties on! If he kept this up, she would soak her sweats in no time. She caught his nostrils flare and knew he could smell her. That pissed her off and turned her on at the same time. She'd never be able to hide how fucking horny he made her.

Thank goddess the drive into White Horse didn't take long. If she had to sit next to him any longer, she didn't know if she could control herself. *What the fuck. I'm not some teenager with exploding hormones. Get a grip on yourself, Billie Cameron.* She nearly jumped out of the truck when he pulled it to a stop.

"I'll be right back," she said, her face flushing pink. *I've finally cracked. That has to be it, I'm losing my ever-loving mind.* Sensory reflexes guided her into the bank without running into anything or anyone, her mind going a million miles an hour. She'd had sex before. Why was *he* different? *AHH!*

"May I help you, Miss?"

She met the eyes of a twenty-something teller. The kindness in her eyes took Billie by surprise. She must look a mess in her current outfit.

"I lost everything but my license. I need to order checks, a bank card, and withdraw some cash for basic supplies."

"I'm happy to help you. May I see your I.D.?"

Billie handed the driver's license to the teller. Her name tag read Sara.

"How much cash would you like Miss Cameron?"

"Um, this is embarrassing. I have no idea. I need to replace my entire wardrobe. We're headed to Oklahoma City to do some shopping. I also need all the basic girl stuff. I lost everything."

"I'm sorry to hear that. We have several sister branches in Oklahoma City, I'll alert them in case you need more cash. Let me start you with five thousand."

Billie had no idea how many clothes that would buy, she rarely bought things for herself. Cayum supplied most of her clothing. He had some weird fetish, dressing her like some kind of fighter Barbie.

The clothes were cool and covered her body, so she didn't give a fuck. She had more things to worry about than clothing.

"I have your bank cards ordered. Shall I send the checks to the address on your license?"

Fuck, she had no idea. Glancing quickly at the license it had a White Horse address. "Yes, that's perfect. Thank you."

"What kind of checks do you want? I can get a catalog."

"Yes, thanks."

Billie looked around the bank, taking in the polished dark wood. The employees looked happy. Each one had a plant or other personal items in their space. The energy felt bright. Something she could get used to, being around positive energy.

She returned every smile with one of her own, enjoying the normal. Normal? What is that? Maybe she'd find out one day. Perhaps even today. She let the smile she felt inside reflect on her face, another first for her.

Sara returned with a large stack of cash and a book with checks she could choose from. Her eyes immediately drew to a small aburn haired beauty holding a book. It reminded her of Ava.

"That one."

"Oh, Belle. I love her. Great choice. I'll get those checks sent out to you overnight. You poor dear. Let me give you a card. If you need anything at all, give me a call and I'll be happy to help."

Billie felt overwhelmed by all the kindness shown to her lately. It all started with Logan picking her up off the side of the road. Weak and at her most vulnerable the last thing she expected was kindness. It scared the fuck out of her. Lady Death went all soft. No, never that name again. I am Death now, and Death doesn't need a gender tag.

Sara handed her the cash with a gold embossed card on top, pronouncing her assistant bank manager.

"I'm filling in for Phyllis, she's on maternity leave. I'm sure you'll meet her soon. Now, if you want something else to wear into the city, you continue down Main Street to Red Row. Turn right to the second shop Tara's Toggs. Tell her I sent you.

"Can I help you with anything else?"

"Thank you. Seriously, thank you, you've been more than kind."

Sara smiled. "It doesn't cost anything to show kindness."

Bless her sweet, naive heart. Billie believed that once. A luxury that she could no longer afford. Now every kindness had to be measured and weighed. Not wanting to put a damper on the woman's enthusiasm, she smiled warmly and thanked her again before leaving the bank.

She felt Logan's eyes on her as soon as she exited the bank. The tightness in her chest eased as she met his eyes. They were raw, honest, and unguarded as he gazed at her. Lust mixed with fascination, and something more. She had that same unnamed something that niggled at her brain about him.

He seemed so familiar, why couldn't she remember? She had a near-perfect memory recall. Scarily, it often played in her head before each kill. A list of her opponents' crimes would flash before her eyes. None of them had been innocent. Each a monster in their own way. Murderers, rapists, child molesters, and worse. She only left the slayer alive to piss Cayum off.

He hadn't ordered a kill because he intended for her to lose the fight. He didn't want her out of her contract. Cayum wanted her under his thumb, under his control so he could continue to exploit her unusual abilities. He underestimated her, then again, he always had. While she learned the first time to never underestimate him.

Billie's eyes remained locked with Viper's as she walked to the Ford Bronco.

She heard him growl as she passed in front of the truck. Good to know she had the same effect on him.

A cocky grin tilted up the left side of her face as she opened the door and climbed inside. Ignoring the obvious sexual tension, she launched into her experience with the teller, ending with directions to the shop.

Viper

His cock grew rock hard the second she stepped from the bank and caught his eyes. The fucking twenty feet walk turned into some slow-mo film moment in his head where they eye fucked each other the entire way. Then she gets in and launches into girlie mode. A new side for sure. Billie didn't talk much. She saved her words. At least from what he'd seen.

The three days she spent sleeping he and Mother reviewed hours of footage. Thanks to his friends' unusual techno abilities they were able to pull footage from around the world. He wasn't trying to stalk her as much as try and figure out how he knew her, and why the memory was blocked.

He needed answers. He didn't know how to broach the subject with Billie. *Hey, I know you're free and just got Ava back and stuff, but we need to ditch the kid and head down to New Orleans to find some seer.* He was pretty fucking positive that approach would go over like a lead balloon.

It's one of the biggest reasons he jumped at a chance to be in a cage with her all day. He needed to know her better. He wanted to know if she remembered something he didn't. Viper had serious doubts about that. If someone blocked his memories, they likely blocked hers too. He had a sneaking suspicion they weren't supposed to even feel recognition. Somehow the bond or whatever drew them seemed to short circuit the magick enough that he knew something wasn't right. Now he needed to figure out if she felt the same way.

Tamping down his hormones, he drove them to the shop. He knew little about the town, having only visited a handful of times in the last few years since Rage started setting up their base of operations.

He parked the truck turning off the engine.

Chapter 15

Death

"I shouldn't be long. I'm going to grab something better to wear."

"Take your time, we have the rest of the day. We can even stay in a hotel if we don't finish up."

"Can I think about that?"

His smile lit up his eyes. "Sure. Why don't I run to the gas station, top off the tank and get road trip supplies?

Her eyes crinkled in amusement wondering what supplies they'd need for a two-hour trip.

"It's a plan."

She shut the door heading for the shop. The brightly lit display showed the latest winter fashion with a summer preview. Billie realized she had no idea what she liked fashion-wise. *Fuck this is going to be harder than I thought.*

Taking a deep breath, she opened the door. A bell jingled above her, alerting the occupants to someone's imminent arrival.

A beautiful brunette with, well, perfect everything greeted her with a soft southern accent.

"Welcome to Tara's Toggs. I'm Tara, how may I help you? "Sara Crawford sent me."

"You must be Billie, that sweet girl phoned me and told me to expect you. Now let me get a good look at you so I know what size to pull."

She looked Billie up and down with a discerning eye muttering "mmhmm" on occasion. Billie felt a bit on guard, usually if someone sized her up that long they intended to launch an attack. Her senses on high alert, she forced herself to remain motionless.

Thankfully, the woman finished. "If you'll follow me to the fitting room, I'll pull a few things for you. Get you a better outfit to travel in. Do come back later when you have more time. I have several styles that you'd look amazing in."

Billie smiled at the woman's enthusiasm, following her to a large brightly lit dressing room. It had a bench seat, a chair, and even a small round table.

"I'll be back in two shakes of a horse's tail."

It took only a few minutes for Tara to return with an armload of clothing. After trying on half a dozen outfits, she decided on an off-the-shoulder, black lace corset top, low-rise jeans, knee-high boots, and a wide belt with metal studs. She also chose a fleece-lined denim jacket.

Twenty minutes later, she stepped out into the street wearing her purchases and carrying her borrowed clothes in a bag with the shop's logo on it. She promised Tara to come back and shop. In truth, if she weren't looking forward to spending the day with Logan, she would have let the woman choose everything for her and be done with it.

"That was fast."

"Was it?"

"You don't know?"

"Cayum insisted on buying my clothes. I don't have a lot of shopping experience."

"I can only imagine what he made you wear."

"Actually it wasn't that bad. He didn't like anyone staring at me unless I was In the ring fighting. The clothes were stylish and expensive. He has a full-time staff that takes care of fashion for all he considers to be 'his'."

"I'm sure between the two of us we can handle clothes shopping. It's not my favorite chore but I break down a few times a year to replenish the wardrobe."

Two massive Big Gulps sat in the truck's cup holders; a paper bag filled with snacks sat in the bench seat by the driver.

She looked at him curiously.

"Are these road trip supplies?"

"You bet. No matter how old you get, road trip food should always look like a ten-year-old has hundred dollars to spend and no parents around to tell him no."

Billie laughed. "Do I want to know what's in here?"

"Only one way to find out." He picked up the bag quickly upending its contents between them before he put the truck in reverse and headed toward the highway.

Her eyes widened as she surveyed the contents of the bag. Three different kinds of chips, jerky, candy bars, jellybeans, and several snack cakes.

"There's no way you'd put all this in your body."

"Only on road trips and cheat days. Plus, wolf metabolism burns it off. As long as I don't eat this stuff all day, every day, I'm not doing permanent damage to my body.

"Hmm."

"What?"

"I was thinking my mimic powers need to borrow your metabolism."

Logan threw back his head, laughing. "Somehow I don't think yours is that far behind mine.

"Maybe, not," she grinned, "but yours is better."

"I could help you work off the calories. If you want."

She suddenly had a mental image of him lying naked in bed covered in snack cakes. After she licked him clean, they could work off those calories. *Down girl.* Billie couldn't help but laugh.

"Shopping first."

"Oh, so sex after shopping?"

She felt her cheeks heat.

"I meant let's focus on the task at hand."

He chuckled. "Task at hand, road food. Please hand me a cherry pie."

Billie rifled through the snack pile, finding that cherry pie. she handed it to him before beginning to put the contents back in the bag. By the time she finished, he'd opened the pie. Taking great pleasure in scooping the contents out with his tongue, a smirk tugging at the corner of his mouth; eyes mostly on the road.

She turned on the radio flipping through the stations until she heard Type O Negative's 'Bloody Kisses'. Billie cranked up the radio singing along while trying to ignore the x-rated pie-eating porn show not two feet from her. At some point, she crossed her legs to keep from squirming.

The trip to Oklahoma City took two hours. At some point, Logan decided to give them both a break, so they started talking about motorcycles. The time went quickly after the sexual tension eased between them.

"What do you think about hitting a department store first? They'll have a variety of items all in one place."

"Good idea. Is that a Montgomery Ward, I see?"

"Yes, shall we start there?

"Yes, definitely."

Once they were inside, Billie headed to the second floor. She picked out bedding for her and some for Ava as well. After loading the purchases into the Bronco, they headed back inside. Billie decided she had to face the music and headed to the women's department.

An hour and several purchases later, she decided to head to a lingerie shop. Her first time visiting one. Something she always wanted to do but didn't want Cayum going through her drawers to see what she purchased.

"You sure you want me to go in here with you?"
Billie turned to look at him, "Yeah, why wouldn't I?"

He chuckled, shaking his head. "No reason."

Thanks to the friendly sales lady in Dillard's, she knew all her sizes. They stopped by there right after Montgomery Ward's. She wandered through the racks, picking up several things to try on. Deciding it was time for a little payback, she slipped into a nude teddy that gave peeks of her skin through sheer side panels. Wide black lace adorned the front of it. The deep vee neck showed off her ample cleavage while the high cut made her legs look longer and hugged the cheeks of her ass.

"Logan, I hate to ask this, but could you ask one of the employees to pick out a pair of heels for me? I want to see what this looks like when I wear some."

His voice, low and thick, asked, "Size?"

"Nine, thanks." She grinned; she'd only just begun to return the tease she endured during the car ride earlier.

A few minutes later someone knocked on the dressing room door. "I have a few shoes for you, Miss."

Billie opened the door wide enough to take the shoeboxes from the clerk's hand. "Thank you."

"No problem and wow. His jaw's going to drop when he sees you in that."

Billie grinned nodding her head, she winked at the clerk before closing the door. She tried on all three pairs before deciding on the nude ones. She liked heels, but never had the opportunity to wear them before. The color should go with several outfits. That way she wouldn't need to buy more shoes.

After today she decided she liked it better when Cayum did it for her, not something she'd ever admit out loud, but the truth, nonetheless. At the last second, she undid the braid and let her long dark hair fall loose down her back. Surprised it nearly reached her hips. With no comb to use she ran her fingers through it one last time gathering the nerve to open the door and show Logan her outfit.

Chapter 16

Viper

He knew she was up to something. It was plain by the time they headed to Dillard's his woman didn't like to go shopping. Maybe they'd give internet shopping a try, Mother swore by it. Viper planned on talking to Blade as soon as he got back. Synne would have information by then and he'd need the VP's okay to take off.

His eyes went immediately to the dressing room door when he heard it open. Viper's jaw gaped open and his cock became hard as steel.

The piece of lace she wore covered her like a one-piece bathing suit, and nearly the same color as her skin save for the decorative black lace. Sheer panels showed off her toned stomach and the curve of her hips.

He looked around before launching himself at her with a low growl. They were in the dressing room door closed with his lips on hers in a matter of seconds.

"Odin's damn, woman you're driving me insane. Just being near you makes me want to be sheathed deep inside that sweet pussy of yours."

He could hear her pulse quicken. The smell of her arousal made it damned near impossible to not take her hard right then and there, employees and customers alike be damned. Viper gripped her perfect ass with one hand pressing her closer so she could feel how much he wanted her.

"What were you thinking?" he whispered hoarsely into her ear.

"I wanted to tease you, as you did me."

He chuckled low and throaty. "Looks like you have better will power, because I don't plan on leaving this dressing room until at least one of us has an orgasm."

Her eyes widened. He loosened his hold slightly, giving her a little space and time to think. Without saying a word, she nodded.

"Can you keep quiet?"

"I have no clue."

"Try."

"What are you going to do?"

Instead of replying, he sank to his knees. His nose in her crotch, he took a deep inhale. "You smell so fucking delicious."

Using his wide tongue and hands he spread her legs before licking her through the material. He heard the moan escape before she cut it off. When he looked up, her eyes were closed, her head laying against the wall.

A smile turned up the corners of his lips. Mouthwatering in anticipation, he found the snaps between her legs that fastened the garment together. He popped both quickly before running a finger from her lower lips to her clit in a smooth motion. Viper brought his finger to his lips sucking her juices off and savoring the flavor. When he glanced up, he noticed her watching him under hooded eyes.

"You taste good too."

She whimpered almost silently; wolf ears picked it up. Encouraged by her reaction, he replaced the finger with his wide, flat tongue licking her slowly a few times before he began to lap at her juices.

Her legs began to shake when he inserted one long finger inside her stroking in and out of her wet folds. He found her clit sucking the bundle of nerves into his mouth then gently rolling it in his teeth. Viper slipped in a second finger curving them to hit her g-spot.

His tongue now danced across her clit before lapping up more of her juices. Long fingers stroking in and out of her. He increased the pace when she started to squirm. Viper was still becoming attuned to her body and sensing her orgasms. Her legs began to quiver, she must be close.

Viper pulled his fingers out, replacing them with his tongue. Tongue fucking her while rubbing her clit. Soon her legs buckled, and he caught her as the orgasm hit her body. He had to give her props for staying so quiet. Normally he wanted to hear his woman moan in pleasure. They could take care of that later.

Death

She lay on the dressing room floor in his arms. The inside of her mouth bled where she bit it to remain quiet. It took her a few minutes to gather her thoughts enough to speak.

"We're getting a room."

"Yes ma'am. Do you want to stop for food or order room service?

"Room service. Let's pay for this stuff and go."

"I'll slip out and meet you by the cash register."

"Okay."

She waited until he left to change back into her clothes. Her knees still weak, she gathered the lingerie she wanted and headed toward check out. If any of the employees knew what happened, they hid it well. Billie let out a sigh of relief when they stepped outside the store. Logan moved all the bags to one hand, intertwining his fingers with hers as they exited the mall and headed to the Bronco.

Less than thirty minutes later, they were on their way to a king suite, complete with a jacuzzi tub. He carried all the bags they'd need for the night while she nervously chewed the inside of her lip. She wished she knew more about sex, how to please him. Billie wanted more than anything to give him the pleasure he gave her. She already had a plan in mind for when they headed back to White Horse tomorrow.

A slow smile spread across her face.

"What are you thinking?"

"You'll find out eventually." Damn, she needed a poker face around this man.

"Is that right?"

"Yes." Her answer came out shorter than intended, but damn he got under her skin fast.

He shrugged it off with a smile. *Oh my god, he's enjoying this.* Now she didn't know if she wanted to fuck him or punch him in the arm for turning her into a mass of raging hormones. By the time they got into the room, she was positively pissy. *When the fuck did, she start having girly emotions?*

Chapter 17

Viper

He sensed her emotions swing. The cocky grin instantly replaced by a look of concern.

"What do you need?"

A concert of emotions played across her face. "Why don't we order room service? It will give us a chance to get to know each other more."

The small smile lit the corners of hazel eyes, chasing away some of the shadows. *Slow your roll. She's been through a lot in a short time.*

Yeah dick, shut the fuck up, and let's listen to our woman.

Viper quickly rifled through the nightstand next to the bed locating the room service menu.

"What are you in the mood for?"

"Something, not junk food."

He laughed. "I get it, you're a good girl and don't break training."

She blanched before quickly schooling her face. "Cayum didn't allow many cheat meals. He didn't want his top athlete getting fat or out of shape."

She surprised him by mimicking the Dark Fae's voice. It would fool an untrained ear. Viper filed that information for later.

"They have prime rib, chicken, and salmon."

"Prime rib medium-rare with all the fixings, and a hot fudge sundae. Oh, and if you don't mind, ask for the hot fudge on the side?"

"You don't like a lot of hot fudge or you like your hot fudge with a little bit of ice cream?"

A pretty blush spread across her cheeks. "Sometimes, when Cayum wasn't paying attention, I'd just eat the hot fudge."

"I'll order extra. Would you like a drink?"

"I'd love some whiskey. You don't suppose they carry Yamazaki, do you?"

"You like Japanese whiskey?"

"I love Japanese whiskey."

"Did you go there for fights?"

"Not often enough; it's where I found Ava. I went for a walk after a particularly brutal fight. I was still cut up and bruised. One of my eyes was nearly swollen shut.

"I caught sight of this bit of pink fluff. Her tiny bunny ears lowered against her head. Tears streamed down her face. It nearly broke my heart."

"What happened to her parents?"

"I found them murdered. Drained of blood." She hopped from the bed clearing her throat. "Order. I think I want a drink. I'm going to grab a soda from the machine then get some Ice. Do you want one?"

"Sure, I'll put in the order."

"Deal."

He watched her pick up the ice bucket and head to the door. She flipped the latch so it wouldn't close and headed out the door. It took everything he had not to go after her. His wolf screamed for him to protect her. Only his training and rational thinking kept him glued to his spot for two full minutes before he called room service. Had he moved before then he would track her down, just to make sure.

Okay order the damn food, get your shit together and figure out why the wolf freaked the fuck out.

After room service was ordered, he focused his senses pushing them outward down the hall and then two floors down where the ice machine was located. At least the one Billie chose to use. He didn't sense any menace. There was no change in her breathing or heart rate. In essence, he sensed no immediate danger. Perhaps the wolf warned him of her past. That made sense. He could only imagine what she'd been through, but he intended to find out.

She came through the door carrying two bottles of classic Coke in one hand and the full ice bucket in the other. A smile turned up the corners of her generous mouth.

"I don't know what made me go down two floors. Mostly I wasn't paying attention when I wandered into the elevator; but hey, it got us two bottles of coke with real sugar."

"Sweet." He forced a little cheer in his voice, concerned a trained fighter would let their guard down enough to not know what floor they were on, or why she headed to the elevator at all. Most floors had an ice machine.

"Food should be here soon. You owe me a story about Japanese whiskey. They didn't have any, by the way. They did have a decent Canadian I thought you might want to try."

"Thanks. Whiskey, like hot fudge, is one of my guilty secrets. I thought about opening my own distillery sometime. 'Death Whisky', the bands would line up to have it at their shows. As would the underground fighting fans. Plus, I'd have my own whiskey. Win, win.

"I spent a few years in Japan training with the best martial arts teachers in the world. Multiple disciplines. Cayum, once he found out about my mimicking abilities, decided I needed to win money for him in the fighting ring. I'd been fighting all my life, only this time I had a roof over my head and someone who cared about me.

"At least I thought he cared about me. I had no idea he was using me, manipulating me until he had use of me."
"How did you meet him?"

"He found me on the streets near Bayou Lafourche and offered to protect me. Offered me a safe, warm bed and three meals a day. The first six months I slept with one eye open, waiting for the other shoe to drop. Waiting for him to be like everyone else. Little did I know Dark Fae excel at the long game.

"He knew the moment I began to trust him. The moment I let my guard down. I had everything I ever wanted; clothes that fit, and new ones at that. From everyone's reaction, they were in style, expensive. Cayum loves expensive things. I had a roof over my head, a bedroom bigger than any house I'd ever squatted in. Three meals a day and snacks if I wanted. Plus, he took an interest in my natural fighting abilities. Said he wanted to train me so I could always protect myself even when he wasn't around.

"No one tried to touch me once Cayum took me in. No more attempted rapes, no trying to steal from me or kill me because they are tripping on some mind-altering drug. For a year, it was paradise. My dreams finally came true."

A loud knock at the door. "Room service."

He touched her shoulder gently as he crossed the room to open the door. Taking the cart, he tipped the delivery boy and wheeled it in himself. Parking the cart by the table, he looked askance to Billie.

"Do you want to eat while it's hot or finish the story?"

"Let's eat, and I could use a two-finger pour of that whiskey."

He smiled, pouring her a glass of whiskey before he began to load the silver domed plates onto the table.

She joined him after she downed the whiskey in one long gulp. He wanted to comfort her, yet he had no clue how. Viper hadn't allowed many women to get close to him. He'd seen Omen's wife disappear and Rage's wife and children get slaughtered. Love wasn't for him. Now his heart ached for her and he wished he knew what to do. *Fuck I'm turning into a pussy whipped sissy.* He'd hear that from at least one of his brothers, he had no doubt.

Death

They ate in companionable silence. The room felt lighter by the time Billie dug into the first silver pitcher of hot fudge with a spoon. An idea began to form in her head with what to do with the second one.

She talked enough about Cayum and her past for one night. There was still that small voice in the back of her head telling her that she couldn't trust anyone. Cayum was the perfect example of that flawed thought. Besides, Logan Haagan was simply delicious, all six feet and six inches of him.

Billie had sex a few times, honestly until the first time with Logan it was disappointing. He ignited something within her. Something she didn't know how to put in words, or hell even thoughts. She didn't want to think right now.

She stood to her feet, a wicked gleam in her eyes as she licked the last of the fudge off the spoon. Surprising herself she walked to his chair straddling him before pulling him in for a kiss.

Their tongues warred for control until both gave into the passion and simply allowed the kiss to deepen on its own. Her hands went behind his head, running her fingernails gently along the back of his scalp, encouraging him closer. When she broke the kiss, her breathing ragged, she looked into his eyes. They swirled golden in color reminding her of a wolf in the darkness. A low growl emitted from his throat.

"Not yet wolf, ladies first."

She stood and grabbed his hand leading them to the bed. "Strip."

She didn't want to get distracted with undressing his magnificent body, so she occupied her mind with stripping off her clothes, then heading to get the last pitcher of hot fudge. The liquid had cooled to lukewarm, enough for a thick pour.

"Lay back."

She stopped at the edge of the bed, watching him position himself on it.

Muscular arms folded behind his head; his thick legs crossed. She'd have to fix that. Billie planned on being between his legs, and since she'd only ever given one other blow job, she needed plenty of room to figure out what the fuck to do.

Billie gave a shaky laugh. "I really have no clue what I'm doing."

"Do what feels good, what feels right for you. There is no wrong or right."

Billie tentatively poured some of the fudge on his stomach, placing the pitcher on the nightstand before joining him in the bed and slowly licking it off his skin. She listened for his responses, for changes in his breathing and heart rate. *Who knew she could put her warrior training to use in other ways?*

Her tongue slid across his belly button before dipping lower. She felt hands in her hair, as he gathered her hair holding it to one side. His voice was barely above a whisper as he commanded, "Look at me, baby."

Her eyes met his, she could see what her exploration had done to him. Not that the massive cock staring her in the face wasn't already an indication. Keeping her eyes locked with his, she slid lower. Finally, taking a deep breath, she tentatively licked the head of his cock, when he drew in a breath, she repeated the action a few more times before sliding the head of his cock in her mouth.

She'd seen porn a few times but had no idea how to swallow his massive cock like the people in the pornos. Instead, she grasped his shaft with one hand beginning to move it up and down while she sucked the first few inches of his cock into her mouth. Her tongue swirled and licked as she went. The movement made it so much more intimate by looking into his eyes while she took him into her mouth.

Just the look he gave her made dampness begin to pool between her legs. Who knew you could get so turned on giving someone else pleasure? Billie's confidence grew and she used her free hand to gently massage his balls.

"Oh, fuck that feels good. Damn baby those lips. Fuck."

Chapter 18

Viper

He let go of her hair. "Fuck, baby. I'm cumming."

It normally took him a lot longer to cum from getting head. Hell, sometimes he didn't cum at all. Billie's mouth and hands had him busting a nut like a sixteen-year-old.

To her credit, she didn't pull away, instead her lips sealed around the head of his cock and she drained him, even licking the last drop of cum from the head of his cock. He guided her back up his body, kissing her deeply, not caring he could taste his cum on her lips.

"That was so fucking hot."

Her eyes lit up. Kissing her again, he flipped her onto her back. "My turn."

"Didn't you have your turn in the dressing room?"

"Nope, I didn't get to hear you scream."

She giggled, relaxing back against the pillows. He kissed her neck, nuzzling the hollow of her throat. One day he would mark his mate there, biting her deeply enough to leave a permanent mark. His mark.

Leaving the hollow of her throat, he trailed kisses down to one of her breasts, rolling the nipple with his tongue before sucking it into his mouth. He drew as much as the soft tissue as he could into his mouth, using the tongue to caress the skin while sucking gently. One hand on either breast, with the thumb and forefinger one the opposite breasts he rolled the taught nipple. She gasped out loud when he pinched.

Viper pinched harder, at the same time barely scraping his teeth across the other nipple. Her back arched, pushing her breasts closer to him, her hips thrusting of their own volition.

"You don't have to be quiet."

"It's still public, kinda."

"It's a hotel, sex is going to happen in several rooms tonight, guaranteed.

Viper went back to his ministrations switching breasts. This time when her breathing became ragged, she began to let out little moans and whimpers. The sexy as fuck sounds had his cock standing at attention. He slipped a hand between her legs, his fingers instantly drenched with her wetness. Instead of moving down, he began to caress and kiss all over her breast. Every inch of skin kissed, licked, and nibbled; he could tell she was close to the edge.

"Cum for me baby."

Viper rubbed the pad of his thumb over her engorged clit while sliding one finger deep inside her. She exploded, her hips bucking, legs quivering. She called out his name, grabbing a hold of his arms. Her grip firm as the orgasm rode her body.

Smiling he trailed his tongue from her breast to her navel, taking time to nip at the perfect indent before sliding lower and burying his face in her sweetness.

"You taste sweet. I could do this for hours."

She whimpered, grinding her hips into his face. Viper used his tongue to fuck her. Using a shifter trick, he lengthened his tongue; rock stars weren't the only ones with long tongues. Using the agile tool to lick as he sucked on her outer lips, he lubricated one finger in her juices before sliding it around her rim. When she didn't resist, he used his pinky to press past the tight muscle and slide up inside her.

"FUCCCCCK!" Billie screamed, as her juices flooded him again.

"Did that feel good baby?"

"Yes."

"Did you like my finger in your ass?

Her cheeks flamed. "Yes," she whispered hoarsely.

"Turn over for me, baby, get on your knees. Put your ass up in the air."

Splayed in front of him with that sweet ass up in the air he longed to bury himself inside that tight channel, but she'd need to be stretched first. He'd wait for another time to take that sweet ass. Checking her wetness again, he slid the head of his cock against her entrance. She whimpered, rubbing up against him.

"Do you want this cock inside you?"

"Yes."

He slid the head in pulling it back out teasing her a few times before sliding inside, she was still too fucking tight for him to slam. With slow, smooth strokes, he worked in and out of her, driving them both to the edge of madness.

"Fuck me."

The lady didn't need to ask twice. Viper picked up speed.

"Harder, faster."

"Are you sure."

"YES."

He picked up more speed surpassing "mortal" man and entering into shifter speed. Billie's moans and cries grew louder the harder he pounded her. His balls slapped up against her as he pounded her tight little pussy. Juice ran down the insides of her legs.

"Oh, fuck yes, Logan. It feels so fucking good. God don't stop."

He continued to pound her pussy relentlessly. "I'm getting close, baby, cum with me."

Viper once again using her juices lubricated her tight rim before sticking his pinky inside her.

"LOGAN." She screamed his name falling over the edge and bringing him with her.

He laid down beside her, pulling her into his arms. Logan's fingers traced the wing tattoo on her back. A beautiful piece of work started at the nape of her neck and ended at the top of her heels.

One day soon he would ask her about it.

Death

The next morning, they showered, checked out, and headed for a healthy breakfast at one of the local diners on the way back to White Horse. This time they skipped the junk food, opting for ice water since they just finished an enormous breakfast.

"Mind if I ask you a question?"

"Go ahead."

"How did you wind up in Lafourche?

She shrugged her shoulders. "One place is as good as the next when you live on the streets."

"What happened to your parents?"

"I don't have any parents."

"What do you mean, you don't know who they are?"

"No, I have no idea who my parents are or what happened to them."

"How long did you live on the streets?"

"Always? I don't know. As long as I can remember."

"Didn't child services try and put you in foster care?"

She shook her head. "I remember being able to walk and talk and being alone. A dark alley that smelled bad. Someone tried to get me, but I hid. Eventually, they went away. That night I found some newspaper and an old box and slept behind the dumpster. It smelled bad, yet I felt safe there."

"How did you hide?"

"It's another gift I have, like mimic, I can hide from anyone by shutting down my biorhythms. The better the tracker, the deeper I can go essentially shutting 'off' until the danger passes."

"How does it work?"

"I pull all my energy slowly into my body. Twice I've dumped my energy depleting myself completely. The first time I slept for over a month."

"Is that how you got away from Cayum's goons the first time?"

"Yes. I crashed my bike. The road burned through my clothes faster than I thought, luckily my mimic power still held on to the slayer's armor-like hide. Once my skin started peeling off as I slid the opposite direction of the bike, it took over, saving my life. When I sensed the Dark Fae near, I expelled my energy like emptying a battery.

"I don't know how long I would have remained hidden until you came along. Should we talk about the repayment now?"

She watched him shake his head. "The repayment is something you will have to discuss with Blade. He's in charge while Omen, our president, is out."

"You guys all seem pretty alpha, do you elect who leads, or take turns?"

"Over the years, Omen became our natural leader."

"How old are you?"

"Near a thousand now."

She swallowed; talk about a May/December romance. Then again, long-lived creatures had become the norm for her. Dark Fae were immortal, they could be killed, but it was rare and needed special weapons or equipment. Billie wondered if it were the same for Odin's wolves.

"You don't look a day over thirty."

He smiled showing perfect white teeth. "Trying to flatter the old man?"

"Did it work?"

"Maybe?"

She laughed. "Only maybe?"

"I might need more convincing."

"Is that so?"

"Indeed."

She'd forgotten about her earlier plan until he said he needed more convincing. Smiling, she unbuckled her seat belt and slid across the bench seat, putting her hand between his legs. She rested it on his upper thigh, below his balls.

"I think I might be able to convince you."

"What are you up to?"

"You'll find out."

Billie slid the palm of her hand over his crotch, feeling it instantly hardened and strain against the denim. With a quick motion, she unbuttoned and unzipped his fly, allowing his hard cock to spring forward.

She positioned her body across the seat with her head in his lap. Billie slid the tip of his cock in her mouth while one hand stroked his shaft.

"Fuck baby."

She chuckled evilly. "Eyes on the road."

"Yes ma'am."

Billie went back to her tender ministrations, licking the head of his cock like a lollipop, sucking it in her mouth then using her tongue to push it back out. Her tongue explored his head licking and sucking gently. At some point one of his hands wrapped around the back of her head holding the base of her ponytail.

She stopped pulling away slightly.

"Ah, ah. Both hands on the wheel."

She heard him swear under his breath, chuckling. She decided to tease him more. Billie rubbed her thumb over the head, massaging the tip. She listened intently as she tried new techniques with her lips and tongue. He seemed to enjoy it all, a few things were more than the others.

Slowly she worked half of his impressive length into her mouth managing not to gag. His groan told her he was close. Her panties were becoming soaked, she loved turning him on. Billie massaged his balls this time taking a little more of him into her mouth before backing up and going faster. She sucked a bit harder, using her other hand to work his shaft.

Billie felt his balls tighten in her hand seconds before his hot, salty cum filled her mouth. She licked every drop before pulling away. Billie tucked his limp cock back inside his jeans, careful not to catch it and his pubes as she buttoned and zipped his pants.

Chapter 19

Viper

After he dropped Billie off to see Ava, he headed to the meeting room. Synne would be meeting him and Blade. The current office/church room used to be the teacher's lounge. A massive worn oak table took up the center of the room with several cushy office chairs surrounding it. They'd left the floor industrial linoleum at least for now.

Blade sat at the head of the table, his feet kicked up, a sharp knife in his hand cleaning his nails. "I see you survived shopping. You smell like her. Is she your mate?"

"Nice to see you too. Do we have ale on tap?

"Mmhmm, mugs, and barrels behind the screen. Get me one?"

"Sure thing. Have you heard from Omen?"

"He's following a lead somewhere in Turkey. The last place Odin's horn was seen."

Viper nodded; they needed the horn to create more wolves. Nevermore than a hundred they'd lost a few over the years and needed to replenish their ranks.

He grabbed two mugs from a shelf, an old-fashioned wooden cask sat on the table. Viper poured two mugs full before heading back to the table. Handing one to Blade, he sat down on his right waiting for Synne to arrive.

"To answer your earlier question, I believe she's supposed to be but there's a block of some kind keeping us from recognizing each other."

"Care to expand on that statement?"

"When I went to Nic to ask for his help I allowed him to peer inside my head."

"I didn't know vampires did that. Most don't."

"He saw a block of some sort. Said I needed a seer to find out a way to break through it. That's a secret I'd like to keep on his behalf. With Omen gone, I asked Synne to find one for me."

"Devil said she was on her way."

The door opened, Synne strolled inside. "Sorry I'm late. Traffic is hell."

"You drove?"

"No, a young Fae learning to transport got in my way."

"How is that even possible? Blade asked.

"I have no idea. One minute I'm stepping through the portal on my way here, the next moment some joker knocks me out over China. Do you mind if I have a drink?

"Help yourself."

She retrieved a tankard of ale, before taking a seat across from Viper.

"I found you, someone, kinda."

"What does that mean?"

"It means that you need to travel to New Orleans and find her yourself. A woman with Marie Laveau's blood running through her veins and eyes the color of the water."

"How many women live in New Orleans that will claim that same heritage for the tourist trade?"

"I have no idea. Strong magick is at work here and she is your best bet at putting the pieces of yours and Billie's puzzle together."
"You can leave tomorrow and take Elvis, Ghost, and Fang."

"You're sticking me with the new kid?"

Blade smiled, tapping the VP patch on his chest. "Membership has its privileges. Besides, the kid is driving me bonkers. You can get him out of my hair."

"You don't have any hair to get him out of."

"Funny, smart ass."

Viper turned toward Synne. "Thanks for getting the information."

"No problem, I'll send you my bill."

He laughed. "I have no doubt. If you'll excuse us, I have something I need to talk to Blade about."

"Sure, see you later."

"Say Synne, would you mind telling Devil to gather everyone for church?"

"Will do, boss man." She winked playfully at Blade before leaving the room.

"What's up, brother?"

"Billie wants to talk to you about repaying Cayum."

"No worries, I'll figure something out. Are you going to tell her all of it?"

Viper shook his head. "As far as I'm concerned it's done. She and Ava are free and that's all that matters. Though I do feel I owe Elvis for stepping up."

"I'm sure you'll find a way to repay him."

Death

"Are you ready?"

"All packed." She indicated her duffle bag. "Are you sure it's okay to delay talking to Blade about repayment?"

"Yeah, we can worry about it when we get back from New Orleans."

"Do you think we can find this woman?"

"I have no doubt we will."

"You think she can help me too? How do I find out if I have the same block you have?"

"She should be able to tell us or guide us to someone who can."

A knock sounded at the door, Billie opened it to see an excited Ava bouncing up and down on the balls of her feet.

"Billie, come quick. You have a package. It's huge. Hurry up!"

She laughed slinging the duffle over her shoulder before following the exuberantly bouncing girl down the hall and out to the back-parking lot. Two large female trolls in uniform stood in front of the massive crate. The smaller of the two at just over seven and a half feet tall had small black horns protruding from her head.

Troll number two is the one that caught her eye and kept her attention and stood over eight feet in height. Black horns curved and curled each reaching over a foot in length. Decorative jeweled black chains hung gracefully from the horns.

Most trolls didn't look like monsters, well the larger males might get confused with a certain superhero. They had various shades of green-tinged skins. Both males and females grew horns. Some of the more impressive males grew tusks.

The larger and more decorated the horns, the higher rank a troll. Many worked as security, bodyguards and served in the Fae military. While most were Seelie or light Fae some were Dark Fae and a few of the truly ghastly ones claimed a sluagh bloodline.

The taller of the two walked up beside the one holding the clipboard and slapped the shorter woman on the back. "See Tezra I told you we were delivering to "The Lady Death.""

"Just Death please." She strolled forward.

The one called Tezra held out the clipboard. "Please sign here for your delivery from Zenobia's customs."

"I'd be happy to. Does Zenobia usually hire your services for delivery?"

The taller troll offered her hand, "I'm Captain Jethia. Zenobia has had a few of her customs hijacked during delivery. She wanted to make sure that didn't happen again, considering the cost of one of her custom vehicles. Pleased to meet you, big fan by the way. I volunteered."

Billie shook Jethia's hand firmly. Troll warriors were fierce. She'd faced a few of them in the ring. One of her earlier defeats came at the hands of a female troll warrior.

"It's an honor to meet you, Captain."

"The honor is all mine. Could I bother you for an autograph?"

"Sure, what do you want me to sign?"

Jethia pulled a black sharpie out of her pocket handing it to Billie before pushing up the sleeve on her left forearm.

"If you could sign it here. I'm getting it turned into a tattoo. I can't wait to tell the rest of the unit I met you."

She couldn't help but smile, even the underground fighting world had fans. Billie signed. Jethia thanked her then pulled out a card. "If you ever need me or our services don't hesitate to call."

"Thank you, Captain. I'll keep you in mind."

Fang, the new kid, didn't waste time busting Billie's chops about having "fangirls".

"Jealous because I have fans or that I could kick your ass?"

"No way you could kick my ass. I mean, you're a woman."

"You have a lot to learn, pup," Viper said putting a hand on the prospect's shoulder, "before you get your ass handed to you, I'd suggest you zip it."

Fang didn't look happy about it, but he zipped his lip. Good thing, Billie would hate to embarrass the young man in front of his peers.

Viper walked up to her sliding an arm around her waist. "Shall I do the honors?"

"Since I seem to be short a crowbar, go for it."

She watched as he flexed his muscles for her before grabbing a hold of one side of the crate and ripping it open. It took him less than a minute to remove the wooden crate from around her bike.

Ava started jumping up and down. "Billie got a new bike. I want to go for a ride."

She chuckled getting the first good look at her bike. The entire bike, custom steel, had one skull for each opponent whose life she'd taken in the ring. Fully aware it was her life or theirs.

The skulls on the tank looked like they were screaming and trying to rip their way out. The air intake, gearheads, and more were all stylized chrome skulls. The black leather seat had a skull embossed on it as did the saddlebags. She had the saddlebags magickally enchanted to hold several times more volume than normal.

Billie would be able to pack a month's worth of clothes or more into them.

A stylized chrome skull helmet sat on the seat.

"Killer bike."

"Thank you." A huge smile on her face, she promised Ava a ride when they came back from New Orleans. Billie gave the girl a hug and kiss before they left. She knew the girl would be safe and have a lot more fun playing video games with Mother than she would be waiting in a hotel room.

"Good thing we're not trying to be incognito."

Billie looked around the group, then shrugged. "I'd say I'd take another bike, but we both know that's not going to happen. I've been waiting for this custom for two years."

"It's a sweet ride. When are you going to let me test it out?"

"Never," she laughed. "Are we ready?

Viper

They stopped at a roadside diner in Shreveport to refuel. Billie's body must still be recovering from her energy dump. He could hear her stomach growling for the last hour. He had the sneaking suspicion she would have continued to ride without saying anything. Viper got the feeling she was used to putting her needs aside and focusing on the task at hand.

From what he'd gathered so far, Cayum was a harsh taskmaster who enjoyed doling out punishments to keep those around him in line. He had no doubt they'd see him again sometime too. He wanted Billie and Ava too bad to give up for money and a bodyguard for the week. Of course, having the queen of the Winter Fae show up had balanced the power on their side.

He pulled to a stop, putting the kickstand in place before removing his helmet.

"Let's get our grub on."

"Fuck yeah, I'm starving."

Viper put his hand on Fang's shoulder chuckling. "Tell us how you really feel."

"Hungry and horny, like always."

"Ahh pup, slow down and enjoy life. You have years, hundreds when you become one of us."

"That's going to be so badass."

"Badass indeed. Why don't you get us a table, give everyone else a chance to stretch their legs? I need to take a whiz."

Billie walked up beside them, repeating what he'd said earlier. "Tell us how you really feel."

He smiled wickedly at her. "I feel like dragging you in the bathroom and fucking you until you scream loud enough the whole place knows my name."

Instead of responding she headed into the diner and straight for the bathroom.

Hmm. Should I?

"Brother, I for one don't want to be front row center when an entire diner breaks out in an orgy," Elvis laughed

"If I recall," Ghost interjected, "you like orgies."

"That was before the invention of junk food."

"Care to explain that?"

"The smell is different, man. Junk food gives off atrocious sex odors. Have you turned into a monk, Ghost?" Elvis replied

"No, my friend, just nursing a broken heart."

"For the last three decades?"

"Fuck you. Let's eat."

Viper watched his brothers exchange with amusement. Elvis had come to them by way of Jamaica half a millennia ago, his hair in short dreads on top and a fade on the side. Elvis changed his hair often, that and the way he danced had earned him the name of the

'King of Rock n Roll' during the fifties. Before that, they called him Cap. He had a beautiful rig. They had that ship for another two decades before she broke apart on the rocks in a storm.

One charismatic mother fucker. If Elvis and Devil ever had a competition to see how many women they could get in bed, he'd be hard-pressed to choose a winner. Where Devil loved to fight, Elvis loved to dance. Good thing Devil hadn't come with him. He already had to deal with a pup who thought he needed to stick his cock in every pussy he saw.

Ghost on the other hand had become a monk for the last few decades. Although Viper hadn't been around him often the last two decades, he still sensed the sadness in his brother's heart. He and Ghost had been close at one time. Then *she* came and pushed them apart. When *she* broke his heart, Viper hoped their friendship would mend. Perhaps this trip would give them a chance at a new beginning.

The tall, broad-shouldered, fair-haired wolf kept his hair styled like the old days. Long braids pulled back into a ponytail, a full thick beard. He preferred simple clothes, mostly jeans and t-shirts. While Elvis never failed to dress in the latest style.

Viper followed them into the diner taking a quick trip to the can before joining everyone else at a large booth. The broad shoulders of Ghost and Elvis took up one side of the oversized booth with plenty of room in between the two. Why not be comfortable when you could shove the kid on the other side with his woman? Thankfully, Fang's shoulders were more swim team and less linebacker.

He slid in beside Billie, his hips meeting hers. To make more room he slid his right arm over the booth behind her shoulders.

"Do you need more room? I can scoot closer to Fang?"

"No," the word came out with way more growl then intended. Ghost raised a brow in his direction while Elvis gave him a wink and shot him a quick thumbs up. "I'm good right here."

She laughed. "I don't mind being close, besides Fang is a ball of hormones. If I scoot closer to him, he'll pop a woody."

Viper laughed out loud. His woman caught on quick. A few hours into the trip and she started busting chops like one of the other brothers.

"Hey, maybe you're not my type."

He cuffed the kid on the back of the head. "Anything with tits and ass that says yes is your type."

"Ha! He got you there," Elvis said.

"Whatever."

The waitress came handing everyone menus before spouting off the daily specials by memory, a perky smile on her face the entire time. The young waitress gave each of them a once over her eyes landing hungrily on Fang. They did not have time for the pup to get his rocks off. He'd have plenty of opportunity in New Orleans.

Unsprisingingly, everyone at the table ordered the daily special, prime rib done medium-rare. The perky brunette took their menus before heading off to turn in their orders and get their drinks. Beer all around.

The food was surprisingly delicious. By the time they finished, Fang and the waitress had already eye fucked the other half a dozen times.

"Not now, pup. There'll be plenty of pussy in New Orleans."

"Hey, nothing wrong with looking."

"Fine but keep it in your pants until we get to our final destination."

"Sure, no problem, I need to take a wicked whiz. Four beers."

Viper slid out of the booth offering his hand to Billie, pulling her up beside him, he slid his arm around her waist.

Fang slid out of the booth, stopping to pull out his wallet. He counted out several twenties and laid them on the table. "Dinner's on me guys, thanks for letting me tag along."

"Meet you outside in five, pup. Don't be late." Ghost growled.

Fang gave him the "yeah I got it" shrug before heading toward the can.

The waitress breezed by picking up the cash Fang dropped. "I'll be right back with your change."

"Keep the change."

Viper rose once again offering his hand to assist Billie from the booth. His brothers were already out of the booth and headed toward the door.

"You think Fang is going to keep it in his pants?"

"Who knows. We are pulling out in five with or without him."

"What's the big deal about him dipping his wick?"

"Mission first, pussy second. Once we get settled into New Orleans, he'll have free time to fuck to his heart's content."

"Makes sense."

Five minutes later, Fang had yet to appear. Viper swung his leg over his bike.

"Kid's late. Let's ride, he can catch up."

Chapter 20

Death

A split second before she started her bike, she heard a woman's scream. Billie engaged the kickstand enacting the magic ward she had installed to protect the bike as she dashed back inside.

The sounds of a fight came from the women's bathroom. Another scream pierced the air, sending diners scrambling. Billie rushed into the bathroom to find two thugs holding the waitress while another two held Fang. A third held a wicked-looking knife.

"I'm going to cut your dick off for touching my woman," the man said menacingly.

"Maybe you shouldn't leave your woman unattended if she's going to fuck some random customer."

All eyes turned to her. Fang used the distraction to wrestle his way loose. Billie's eyes never left the knife, the man turned waving it at her. Furious she interrupted him.

She stepped forward, faking a stumble before striking the wrist that held the knife. It clattered to the floor. Billie pressed the advantage, taking out the guy's knee. She turned quickly, eyeing the thugs that still held the waitress.

The entire thing happened quickly, leaving the less than brilliant thugs with their mouths agape. Billie took a hold of the waitress's hand. "You best get out of here."

"I'm not going anywhere. What did you do to him?" she shrieked rushing over to the guy on the floor.

She located Fang, who finished knocking the second guy out. "Let's roll." Billie noticed each man wore a cut like the one Logan wore, only they belonged to the Swamp Devils.

Fuck. Without waiting for a response, she grabbed the kid by the arm and half dragged him outside. Viper and the others pulled back in, having ridden off, unaware she didn't follow. It took less than five minutes for her to make her way back in the diner and back out to the bike with Fang in tow.

She made eye contact with Logan. "Fang-face decided to fuck one of the Swamp Devils' old ladies. They're bad news."

"Cat's out of the bag now. Let's roll. We can deal with this better from New Orleans."

The rest of the trip went without incident. Viper canceled the hotel reservations and had Mother find them a house on the outskirts of town to rent instead. A house would be more defensible should they run into any problems with the Devils. Viper insisted she take the master bedroom with the ensuite bathroom.

Billie made immediate plans to buy some bubble bath tomorrow and test out the enormous sunken tub.

Having arrived well after dark, Elvis and Ghost went to get food for the night, while Viper took Fang for a walk. She didn't envy the kid. Logan was none too happy since he specifically told the boy to wait.

She unpacked her belongings before puttering around the old house. The place was huge and at least a hundred years old. From the looks of it, the owner finished having the place remodeled. It didn't look like the type of house that one would normally rent, she wondered how Mother managed it?

All in all, the place had eight bedrooms, six full baths, and two half baths. The enormous kitchen made her wish she knew how to do more than microwave. She'd wondered over the last few years, if she had found Ava under different circumstances would she have made a good mom? Then again, she'd grown up without a mother or a father, how would she know how to raise a child?

Elvis and Ghost arrived with bags of food, the smell causing her stomach to rumble. "Do you guys need any help?"

"Sure, do you want to unload everything on the table? I'm going to look for plates and silverware," Elvis said, offering her his bags.

Ghost sat the bags on the table. "I'll go find Viper and the pup."

Billie began unpacking five large bags of food. The large table was quickly filled with various kinds of sandwiches, pasta, and seafood dishes. Everything smelled delicious, but damn why was she hungry all the time?

Because you're not following your training schedule eating routine. Duh! Damn her inner voice could be a real bitch. It was however the truth. She normally spent her days training her muscles or training to fight, both requiring she eat several meals a day to keep up with her metabolism. Though she hadn't been working out, she hadn't been eating at regular intervals either. Like every couple of hours. At least five times a day, sometimes up to eight times.

While the energy boost Logan, Devil, and Synne gave her went a long way to restore her core, she still felt a "quart" or two low. Her choices were either sleep or she needed to get back on her clean eating schedule. Tomorrow she'd head to the store, or rather find one that did meal prep. Cayum always supplied her food, the best money could buy and prepare. If nothing else, she could at least get supplements and juice. *The best juice is fresh juice.* Corny but true.

"Looks like we're cave manning it tonight unless they packed plates, utensils, and napkins."

"There are a few sets, maybe enough for each of us. I honestly didn't count, no plates, and a ton of napkins. Even a few bibs from the seafood place. Why do I foresee Fang needing one?"

Elvis laughed. "That pup is a mess."

"How did he come to be a part of the wolves?"

"Fang had no idea he was a shifter, not until his eighteenth birthday. He was out partying with friends and shifted. Our brother Seider, I'm sure you will meet him soon, was out on a run when he heard the screams. Seider was able to get Fang away from the scene. Luckily, he didn't kill any of his friends, but a few will have permanent scars."

"They had to fake his death. Local police chalked it up to a rogue wolf attack and Seider brought the pup to live with us."

"Tough break. Still needs to get his head out of his ass, or rather learn how to keep his dick in his pants."

"I have no doubt brother Viper will set the boy straight. What are the chances of the Devils identifying either of you?"

"If one of their old ladies works there, I'd say one hundred percent. Plus, my bike doesn't exactly blend in. Sorry about that."

"It's not like you knew you'd be running with the wolves when you ordered that piece."

"True."

"Our brothers are headed this way."

"You can hear them?"

"Wolf."

"Impressive."

He gave her a mock bow, "Always."

"Elvis, stop making eyes at my woman."

Billie glared at him. While she liked the idea, he hadn't run that tag by her. "I don't see your name stamped on my ass."

Viper

His wolf came immediately to the surface when he saw Elvis flirting with his woman.

"That can fucking be arranged," he growled walking to her side.

"Is that right?"

"Yes!"

She turned to face him looking him in the eyes. "I don't belong to anyone. Got that? Cayum owned me once, never again."

Billie turned on her heel, grabbed something from the table, and stalked out of the room. A hand on his shoulder stayed him.

"Her wounds are still fresh from Cayum. Have no doubt her feelings run as deep as yours, but you must not let your wolf go all caveman."

He let Ghost's words sink in.

"I'm sorry, brother."

"No, I'm the one that should apologize. You didn't do anything wrong. The sooner we find this seer, the sooner we can get this fucking block removed and I can get my head on straight were Billie is concerned.

"I also think we need to hire a witch or two to fortify defenses. I heard rumors of the Swamp Devils, not all of them are sleepers, and at least a few are demons."

Elvis whistled, "Damn boy I hope that pussy was good."

Fang looked like someone punched him in the face. "I'm sorry. I didn't understand how bad I fucked up until Viper told me. I'll keep my dick to myself from now on."

"Yeah like that will happen, we'll let you know when and where you can hunt for pussy after we take care of business. Anyone up for a midnight graveyard tour? Elvis said

"Aren't those just for tourists?" Fang replied scoffingly.

"Only for those not in the know."

"Let's eat. Then I'll go apologize to Billie for being a giant ass and we can head out on a tour."

They made short work of the food eating out of the containers and making use of the plethora of napkins. Viper left his brothers to finish while he went in search of Billie. Following her scent, he found her outside on a bench under a large oak tree.

He waited until she looked up to speak.

"I'm sorry. I didn't mean to imply I owned you. I got jealous when I saw Elvis flash that smile at you. I know what that smile does to women."

She burst out laughing. Not the reaction he expected.

"While I think your brothers are all attractive, none of them pique my interest. Not the way you do."

"Oh." It was all he managed to say before he shut his mouth. She didn't need him spilling all his thoughts on to her. Not now anyway. He smiled, closing the distance between them. He pulled her from the bench into his arms for a sweet kiss.

"In the mood for a graveyard tour? Elvis says there are usually paranormals along the way hiding among the sleepers."

"Sounds intriguing. I'd love to go. Tomorrow we need to go food shopping. Get some healthier options."

"We can do that. What do you like to cook?"

"I don't know how to cook."

"Not a problem, what do you like to eat?

She laughed, going down a list of foods she normally ate. They talked amicably all the way to the garage where they met with the rest of the brothers.

"I hate to say this, but I think I'll rent a Jeep tomorrow. It will be easier to haul what we need and if we need to go in a group without the motorcycles."

"Bite your tongue woman," Ghost said, keeping his face neutral for all of five seconds before he cracked a smile. "Cages are for animals. We like our freedom."

"I can strap you to the roof?"

"If you can get me up there, go for it."

Viper eyed his brother. He hadn't seen him this playful in years. Maybe because Billie was safe. The Brothers didn't go after each other's mates.

"I'll sell the tickets and pup can make the popcorn," Elvis joined in.

His brothers had Billie laughing. The earlier anger was completely gone now. He could see the ease in her shoulders and the building camaraderie. He realized Billie had spent most of her time in the company of males. He made a mental note to ask if she had any friends that she might want to talk to, now that she retlred.

Chapter 21

Viper

The tour started in front of the LaLaurie Mansion. Dark energy roiled from the mansion. The woman tortured her slaves, conducting medical experiments on them, and even inviting her guests to join in the debauchery. It reeked of Evil. No amount of cleansing could clear that energy.

After a few more haunted buildings the tour headed to the St. Louis cemetery. The guide touted it as the most haunted cemetery in New Orleans. He had no doubt restless spirits lived everywhere in the city. The city's layout, perfect for carrying the breeze throughout allowed the spirits to move about easily.

Halfway through the tour, his senses pricked. From the corner of his eye, he caught red eyes peering out from the darkness several feet from their current spot. Whatever it was, followed them as they moved through the cemetery. Soon one pair became two, then four. They were up to six by the time they reached a well-known grave. He tuned in long enough to pick up Marie Laveau. Several people on the tour stopped to leave offerings. Some of them marking the grave with three x's in chalk, others knocking on the grave three times.

Viper would find out the correct way to leave the offering and ask her spirit to help them find the seer they needed. One of her direct descendants. He used a hand signal to get his brothers' attention, before reaching for Billie's hand.

Viper led them off to one side while the stragglers still milled around the famous grave. New Orleans didn't bury their dead, the water table was too high. This led to small cities of mausoleums and monuments. It also leads to an excess amount of preternatural energy. That leads to ghouls.

"We have visitors. The sleepers need to be protected and moved swiftly out of the area. Fang go with Billie and make sure the sleepers get out. You'll need to use your alpha energy boy. So, don't be fucking around. Compel them to leave."

"Yes sir."

"Brothers, you're with me. Let's go distract those ghouls."

He stayed long enough to see Fang reluctantly go with Billie. The kid wanted to see the action, he understood, but the kid needed to understand more. Kicking ass isn't the only thing a wolf needs to know. To be a true alpha you protect the weak first.

The three brothers took three different directions, and he went South. Elvis headed West while Ghost took North. East, he hoped, would be clear. So far, the ghouls, at least that's what he suspected they were, had been following them, and not waiting for their arrival.

Not five yards into the darkness he heard the first wail of a ghoul their call not quite a howl, more like a sound you'd hear at the wailing wall in Jerusalem. He'd been there several times. The eerie sound never left your soul. The sound of grief forever implanted by the sound of their sorrows.

He kept walking, allowing several of them to come closer. Close enough, they'd think they had him surrounded. He doubted any of them dealt with shifters regularly, much less one of Odin's wolves. Viper wasn't cocky, he'd lived centuries of experience on how much damage one of his wolves could take and dish out. He understood why they were limited to only a hundred members.

Viper waited until the first ghouls rushed him before using his preternatural speed to move out of the way. The ghouls collided in a spectacular rush of limbs. Ghouls were not particularly bright. Even so, that would be worth a chuckle or two later around a fire with his brothers.

He felt oddly free standing in the middle of a graveyard with flesh-eating monsters eyeing him for a meal; and he felt better than he had in decades. Here in the darkness in the middle of a city of the dead, he could be his true self. One of Odin's own.

Fuck, he thought a few seconds after he started to shift. He didn't have on a set of his ritually dedicated clothing. The clothes would shift with him, in essence, stored in a dimensional pocket, then when he came back to human form they would reappear. These clothes, minus his cut, ripped to shreds as his body grew nearly double its original height.

Once upon a time when he first learned to shift you could hear his bones snap, break, and watch them reform and lengthen. See them twist. The shift is painful, but the gifts that came with it were more than a fair price to gain in return. Now through time and power, his shift was smooth, swift, and pain-free. Or perhaps he became so used to the pain it no longer registered on his scale.

It's what made him decide to send Fang with Billie. The kid's shift would still be painful, and he'd just learned to control the hunger after his shift. Keeping the wolf's need to eat under control. A shifter's brain still held onto some human aspects even as a wolf. In battle form, they equally held both animal and human components. Completely integrated using the best of each to combine the ultimate fighting machine. A new shifter that hadn't learned to integrate both fully, the human brain often turned hunger into a rage to understand what was going on. It's why most killings happen. Complete accident. Many of those from cursed shifters, most of whom never learn to integrate. They don t get the benefits of a true shifter. Long lives, regenerative cells. They heal faster than a normal sleeper, but nothing like a shifter. Many go mad and don't live long after they're cursed.

The ghouls had regained their feet and were charging him en masse. He dove for the one in the middle, taking them all by surprise. One large, clawed hand wrapped around the ghoul's throat, squeezing the life from him while he positioned for the next attack.

Once clear, he quickly snapped the ghoul's neck before using his other hand to rip it's head off. He didn't remember all the "undead" that came back unless you removed their heads. Better be safe. After pulling the head off, he tossed it at a group of three ghouls who quickly began fighting over the head. He used the body as a shield to bash two more ghouls while kicking a third who tried to bite his leg.

Throwing the body at the two he knocked off balance, he quickly finished off the one he kicked before turning to face more oncoming ghouls.

So far, he'd seen over a dozen since leaving his brothers. Unless all of them headed his direction, there seemed to be an overabundance of ghouls even for a graveyard this big.

If the ghouls didn't eat each other, negating the need for population control, the preternatural community would take care of it. Ghoul attacks were bad press and could be hard to explain to law enforcement. The community liked to keep them under wraps. The sleepers were nowhere near ready to share their world with the things they thought to come from movies and books. Things "man" dreamed but were not real. Oh, they were real.

He'd seen it happen over the centuries: as technology took hold and magick shrank, so did the sleepers' tolerance for anything different from them. Viper had seen one too many witch hunts, vampire staked, et cetera. Only most of the time, some innocent sleepers paid the ultimate price, having no clue what they'd done.

The ghouls came at him almost faster than he could take them out. He even broke a sweat. He dealt with enough numbers that eventually a few got in a good bite or claw. Nothing he couldn't heal but it always stung like a fucking paper cut. Annoyed the fuck out of him.

Viper didn't know how much time went by before the ghouls stopped coming. He looked around noticing bodies piled in the walkways behind him, a gruesome path indeed. He paused long enough to catch his breath and focus his hearing.

Death

She could tell the kid wasn't happy, but she knew the importance of getting the innocents to safety. Her senses pricked as some of her abilities automatically kicked her. Her warrior senses on high alert as they follow slightly behind the end of the group.

"What are we going to do to get them out of here?"

"Seider told me I'm an alpha. I guess all the wolves are. Anyway, he's had me practice my abilities. One of them is being able to send suggestions to sleepers. In this case an urgent need to leave the graveyard immediately, I hope."

"I'm looking forward to meeting Seider, Viper speaks highly of him. What do you need me to do?

"I'm not sure, think of something to spook them maybe?"

Hmm, what can I do to spook someone? She smiled knowing exactly what she'd do.

"Give me two minutes to get to the front of the group since there's no clear path, then use your ability."

"Okay."

He took her at her word, and she turned walking into the edge of the darkness using her honed skills to easily navigate the darkness. One of her sensei's taught her how to blind fight. You simply used your other senses. Billie used her skill to silently navigate around all the sleepers that had been in front of her. Hoping to funnel them further East toward the exit.

She positioned herself a few feet in front of the guide using her hiding abilities to remain unseen until the guide was only three feet in front of her. When she suddenly "appeared," half a dozen people shrieked. Fang must have used his ability. The original screams sent off a chain reaction and the sleepers all but stampeded out of the graveyard and into the tour bus.

Billie followed them through the gates double-checking to make sure there were no stragglers before she headed back into the graveyard. Fang waited for her.

"Which direction should we go?"

"Let's double back. Can you use your hearing to find them?"

Fang smiled at her, "Good idea."

"I'll follow you."

Billie followed behind Fang extending her senses as far she could while keeping track of Fang. He headed North. A scant few yards into the darkness, a large group of creatures headed toward them. What may have once been human had grayish-green skin, razor-like claws, and sharp teeth. They squatted instead of walking upright, their teeth gnashing.

She had no Idea what they were. Only that Fang needed time to shift, and she needed to distract them.

"I'll distract them while you shift."

She saw the hesitation cross his face before he nodded his head. "Thanks."

"I'm sorry." She muttered out loud as she jumped nimbly onto one of the tomb's rooftops. Billie could come back during the day and leave an atonement for disabusing what belonged to the dead.

Hopping from roof to roof until she was a few yards away from the group, she jumped up and down yelling, "Come on you ugly motherfuckers. Come get me."

While a few of them turned her direction too many headed toward the kid as he shifted.

Looking around Billie spotted several chunks of stone on the ground. She hopped down grabbing handfuls before flinging them at the creatures. Billie aimed at the front of the group farthest away from her. She picked out the largest aiming for his head.

The creature howled, turning its gnashing teeth toward her. Red eyes narrowed. A wail like moan emitting from its maw it finally turned and headed her direction, the rest of them following.

Billie once again apologized as she leaped upon the nearest roof. She started leaping from roof to roof, slowly at first. Giving the creatures time to scramble on the roof and make chase. Her speed increased after a few of the creatures made it onto a nearby roof. The bigger one was hot on her heels. She picked up more speed, nearly sprinting from rooftop to rooftop. The only problem is the graveyard was not laid out in any order, which included the height and width of each structure.

She estimated the fastly approaching gap to be seven or eight feet. Billie had no idea if she could make it or not, but she intended to give it her best shot. Adding a boost of speed at the last minute she leaped. Falling a few inches short, the gap was wider than she expected. Billie grabbed the roof, clinging on to it as she scrambled to get back on her feet and away from the creatures until Fang finished shifting and could help her out.

Pain shot up her calf as the leader of the pack clamped down on it. Billie managed to kick him in the face hard enough so she could scramble the rest of the way onto the roof. The wound stung, no doubt filled with bacteria, possibly poison. *Well fuck.*

This time when the big guy came at her, she was prepared. As he came up over the roof, she kicked him in the jaw. She heard a satisfying crunch before moving on to the next roof. She heard another scrambling to get up.

A howl split the air a few seconds later. Relief washed over her. They weren't out of danger, but the odds got a whole hell of a lot better. She spotted Fang headed toward her and motioned for him to head to an open area.

Billie leaped off the roof close to Fang. They'd be able to fight back to back as the creatures came at them.

Her arms and legs suffered several cuts and bruises before her mimic power kicked in, covering her skin in a thick hide before her nails grew into razor-sharp claws. She had no idea how long it took; they were both out of breath and bloody before the creatures stopped coming.

Billie and Fang leaned against each other still back to back catching their breath. Moments later, Viper stepped out of the darkness followed by Ghost and Elvis.

She'd never been so happy to see him; before she could think about it, she ran to him, throwing her arms around him and pulling him in for a kiss. His arms wrapped around her, deepening the kiss. The rest of the world slipped away for a few minutes while celebrating victory in the arms of her lover.

Viper

"You lost your clothes."
"Mmhmm, I forgot to do the ritual when I bought them."
"Looks like you're not the only one."

Chapter 22

Viper

"Dude, put that thing away."

Viper laughed. "Don't be jealous, boy."

He was thrilled to see both Billie and Fang mostly unharmed, though he did smell the ghouls' venom running through Billie's body. He had no idea the extent of her healing abilities. What he did know is that there were far too many ghouls in the graveyard for it to be a natural occurrence.

"Too many ghouls for this to happen naturally. Let's get out of the cemetery."

"That's what those things are, ghouls?"

"Yes, their claws and teeth have venom. Is your system going to need help fighting it off?"

"I don't know. I'm used to fighting one opponent. I've dealt with venom before but not from so many."

He took her hand and began leading them out of the graveyard. At some point Billie stumbled into him, he caught her before she hit the ground.

"Elvis, who do you know that can help?"

"I'll make some calls."

"I'll go find us some wheels."

Viper didn't care how the pup obtained the wheels as long as it got them where they needed to go. He carried Billie out of the cemetery with Ghost on his six. Elvis had difficulties getting reception until they stepped out of the cemetery.

Viper heard him make a few different phone calls. Billie was starting to sweat, her body running a fever.

A few minutes later, they were on the road in a late model truck. Fang rode in the bed, Elvis drove. Ghost rode shotgun and Viper sat in the backseat of the double cab holding Billie. Fang managed to find pants and a shirt that fit him and a pair of sweatpants for him.

Elvis pulled the truck to a stop. A woman with long dark hair and the most unusual eyes gold encircled in emerald green, met them. She ushered them around the back and up a set of stairs.

"Please bring her in here. I'll see what can be done."

She indicated a black velvet chaise lounge the room looked like Victorian Gothic meets Hollywood vampire. Viper laid Billie carefully on the chaise moving out of the way.

Viper stood back watching the woman work. Elvis stepped up to stand beside him. "If Serena can't fix her, she'll know someone who can."

"Hmm. The ghoul venom seems to be suppressing her healing ability."

"She can mimic other abilities. As far as I know, it's compulsory."

"Did she take on any of the ghoul's abilities?"

Fang stepped forward, "Yeah she grew the claws at some point."

"It's possible the mimic ability is trying to incorporate the venom somehow. I don't think I can help. We need to remove the poison from her body. The long way would be a complete blood transfusion. I don't think she has time. Vampires could do it more efficiently, plus when the blood is sucked out the vampire can give her a small amount of blood to boost her healing."

"My closest vampire contact is in Oklahoma."

Serena smiled softly. "No worries. New Orleans is lousy with vampires. It's easy for them to move about the city.

"I'll contact the city's Amir. You know it will come with a cost."

"It always does."

"Julian will deal with you honestly, if for nothing else as a favor to me.

"First you two need better clothes. You can't meet the Amir like that."

"Do you have suggestions?"

"If you have cash, we'll do an exchange."

Viper looked at her.

"I'll get you into a shop. Take what you need. I'll show you where to leave the cash."

The police side of his brain wanted to know more, but they didn't have time for that.

"Let's do it."

"Elvis, load her into the van and pull it around front. We'll be back in a few minutes."

Elvis followed directions, pulling into an old plantation outside the city. Energy washed over them as they passed through the wards of the property. After Billie was taken care of, he would ask Serena about warding the rental place or giving him a referral.

Like much of the area, Viper felt the restless spirits of the dead as they pulled down the oak-lined drive. A small group of people waited for them on the steps. Two men and a petite woman.

Once the van stopped, Fang opened the van door and hopped out to help Viper with Billie. The kid was as helpful as possible since the deal at the diner. Plus, he and Billie fought side by side earlier. That built a kind of camaraderie you couldn't get anywhere else.

The dark-haired man glided forward, yeah vampires' movements mimicked more a glide than a walk, no trick of the mind needed. Serena met him.

"Thank you, Julian. I'm sorry to disturb you."

"You never disturb me, belle. I'd like to see the woman. I need to know how far the poison has spread."

Viper stepped up to Julian, Billie cradled in his arms. The vampire paused less than a foot away and his movements became still. Viper had seen it dozens of times, but it was still weird to see all the animation go out of something. Vampires could become as still as a statue.

"We will have to bargain later, mon ami. The poison is near her heart."

"Do what you need to do. I'll make good on whatever is needed."

Fang stepped up quickly followed by Elvis and Ghost. "Us as well."

Julian's face remained unreadable. "If you will pass her to me, please. My friends and I need to draw the poison out immediately."

Viper reluctantly placed Billie in his arms. He saw Julian turn toward the plantation house then his movements became a blur; when his eyes came back in focus the porch stood empty.

Serena placed a hand on his arm. "Come, I know where they've taken her. She's in good hands. Though to be honest I didn't know Lucien was here. He can be an ass when it comes to barter price."

"Saving her is the only thing that matters. We'll figure something out."

"I have no doubt, Odinson."

She led them into the house and the door opened by a gaunt-looking man of undeterminable age. The man reminded him of the eerie old black and white movie butlers. Complete with the bass voice and the "Come in."

Serena didn't pause or explain her actions, instead she took them directly to the wide sweeping staircase, down a hall, and up another staircase to the third floor. Down a long, candlelit hallway to a set of double doors. Billie lay on a blood-red crushed velvet chaise lounge with three vampires around her. Julian laid her against his chest while he drew the poison from her neck. The blonde male vampire held one wrist carefully in his hand, while the female, a redhead, held the other similarly.

He fought the urge to rip them away from her. *Calm the fuck down wolf.*

OURS! the wolf growled at him.

Smell the poison, look at her she's not healing. The massive dark head of his wolf came into his peripheral vision. It's glowing golden eyes looking over every inch of their woman. Once he was satisfied, he chuffed and strolled away.

It took the vampires nearly an hour to clear all the poison from the ghoul's venom. Which meant Billie needed more vampire blood than they originally thought. The only good news was each vampire gave her as little as possible. Drinking too much of a vampire's blood gave them some power over you. How much depended on the vampire, both their skill and their power level.

Death

"Fuck my head hurts. Fang, did you drop me on my head?"

Suddenly her warrior reflexes kicked, and she opened her eyes to take in my surroundings. Logan, Ghost, Elvis, Fang, and some woman she didn't know stood loosely around her.

She sat bolt upright before realizing each of her wrists were held in an iron grip. A set of hands firmly on her shoulders. A voice whispered in her ear, "Relax we mean you no harm."

Tension instantly eased out of her body. Logan moved into her vision. Should she be laying on some guy's chest? Shouldn't her boyfriend be going all wolf?

"Hey," he said, bringing his hand up to cup her face. "Welcome back."

"Welcome back, did I go somewhere?"

A look of concern crossed his face. "What's the last thing you remember?"

Billie started to get up again until that soothing voice spoke again.

"Non, mon ange tu n'es pas' encore prêt."

She did feel a little dizzy, staying put seemed solid advice, but why did he call her angel? Her mind still felt fuzzy. What did she remember?

"Ghouls. The pup and I kicked a lot of green ghoul ass."

"Hey, you're not that much older than me."

A smirk curved the corner of her mouth. Then a new memory surfaced. "Oh god, I saw him naked."

Laughter erupted around her.

"Now, sit up, beauty. I think you will feel better."

"Can someone explain where I am, whose chest I'm on? Something?"

She felt the man's chest rumble with laughter as he eased her into a sitting position.

"Forgive us, we are all made daft by your beauty."

Boy, this guy is laying it on thick. Not a good sign.

"Logan?"

"I'm right here, babe. The ghoul's venom poisoned your system. We had to ask for some assistance to remove it from your blood."

"What kind of assistance and I should have been able to heal."

"Before you passed out, you said it was the first time you were struck by more than one venomous creature at the same time. We brought you to a witch first when she couldn't help, we enlisted the aid of a vampire friend."

VAMPIRE! Billie shot up from her seated position, moving as far away from everyone as fast as she could, her heart beating fast enough it felt like it would burst through her chest with each increasingly painful beat.

Vampires terrified her. Cayum often used them to punish her.

Chapter 23

Viper

He smelled her fear. It poured from her, filling the room like perfume. A perfume for predators and she was in a room full of them.

Julian started to speak.

"It might make it worse. Give me a few moments please."

"I can only speak for myself and those under my jurisdiction. That does not include Lucien or Velvet."

"Are you trying to insinuate that your two best friends cannot contain their baser urges?" the petite redhead asked.

"*Non*, just that you are not under my purview."

"Accepted, for now."

"Can we allow the wolf to tend his mate?"

The word reverberated through his head he expected it to stick. To click, but it didn't. He approached Billie cautiously speaking soothingly.

"Billie, does Cayum employ vampires?"

"Yes."

"Did he use them against you?"

She shuddered. "Yes."

He closed the distance between them, gathering her up in his arms. She trembled as he held her, and he wondered what Cayum had allowed the vampires to do to her. She was clearly terrified.

"Can we leave?"

"Not yet. We have to negotiate their fee."

Her eyes grew wide. He registered Serena's presence.

"Perhaps I could be of assistance. Billie, my name is Serena. I'm a friend of Elvis'. May I take you into another room or even outside if you wish while they finish?"

"Are there other vampires here?"

"Yes."

"Can you take me somewhere else?

"Yes, of course. Don't worry, Wolf, I'll keep her safe. Julian, I'm taking a car."

"But of course, *cherè*."

Viper watched a woman he didn't know lead his woman out of the bedroom. Elvis stepped up beside him. "Will your witch friend keep her safe?"

"My witch friend is a sorceress of some renown. Billie is safe."

Viper turned around to face the vampires. "We're ready to barter."

"Come and join us for dinner. I hate to negotiate over an empty stomach. Plus, you're guests, please come enjoy my hospitality."

Viper knew it would be useless to demand they get it over with. Vampires, even the decent ones, loved to play games.

"Please, give us a moment, my brothers and I need a few moments to converse."

Julian bowed his head. "Of course."

The vampires swept out of the room. He turned to Fang, knowing the vampires would most likely hear him.

"Take your cues from Ghost, Elvis, or myself tonight. Have you ever been around vampires?"

"No."

"Vampires love games of all kinds. Everything's a game or test of some sort. Each action and reaction must be measured carefully. This is as important as the advice I gave you in Shreveport."

"Understood, I won't let you down."

Viper followed the coppery scent of blood to what could have been a ballroom now turned into a dining hall. A massive antique oak table took up the center of the room. Nearly two dozen beings sat around the table, he knew many of them were vampires, but not all.

Looking around, he didn't see an immediate source for the blood. On alert, he walked toward the head of the table where Julian sat. One of the vamps he'd met earlier on either side.

Julian stood up, "Welcome honored guests. Please be seated. Ladies and gentlemen, we are honored to have four of Odinsons with us tonight." He then pointed to each of them giving their names before he quickly rattled off the names and titles of the rest of the guests around the table. He took special note of those who were from the vampire council.

Viper took a seat, Fang sat next to him, while his brothers sat directly across from them on the other side of the table. The blonde vampire, Lucian, sat next to Ghost while the redhead, Velvet, sat on his right.

"We were getting ready to dine. I do hope you enjoy the festivities."

Julian picked up an empty crystal goblet, using his knife to strike it making a tinkling sound to draw everyone's attention.

"In honor of our special guests from Europe, we have a special treat for you tonight."

"Alec, if you will please do the honors."

A regal-looking man with dark hair wearing clothes from a few centuries past stood up giving a short bow before heading off into another room. Julian clapped his hands, several wait staff immediately emerged placing a silver domed plate in front of him and any other non-vampire in the room. Empty crystal goblets sat in front of each vampire.

Viper had the sneaking suspicion he wasn't going to like what was about to happen. He quickly sized up the room, wondering if they could get the pup out before one of the ancient vampires eviscerated him. Even with three of Odin's wolves, or Odinsons as they were referred to in the preternatural community, he didn't know if they could win. Fang would help out, but the pup had not yet begun his journey into godhood; nor could he until the horn was found. At least a dozen old vampires and a few ancients sat around the table. Not to mention the other shifters of various kinds and at least two of demon blood.

Demons smelled like rotting meat gone rancid. A smell you don't forget if you live to remember it. Fang remained silent beside him and a cursory glance told him the kid's mind was going a million miles an hour. So far, the kid had managed to keep his face schooled.

Alec returned, followed by two men. Each man had a black hood over their face. Their hands were bound behind their backs. Two vampires escorted each. Alec could have no doubt handled them, so the extra muscle was purely for show. He, unfortunately, had to deal with the council before.

The council of thirteen vampires from various European countries governed vampires around the world. Whatever they said went. To go against the council meant final death, and usually, in the most painful way, the council could dream up. His gut instinct screamed at him to get up and leave the table with his brothers, but he knew they had to stay until the negotiations were finished and a trade deal signed. That's how vampires worked. Normally you negotiated before the vampire rendered the task.

Twice now he'd given an oath to a vampire on Billie's behalf without knowing the final deal. She was either his fated mate or he'd lost his mind. The block must be rendering the mating recognition null and void. After they dealt with this and got some rest, he would find the seer and figure out the next move.

Once the group arrived at the table the captives' legs were bound together before they were lifted to the top of the table. A large metal hook with a cable attached was inserted in between their leg bonds before they were lifted off the table and left to dangle in mid-air.

Liveried servants placed a large crystal punch bowl under each man.

Chapter 24

Viper

A cool hand on his arm drew his attention. Velvet's small hand lay on his arm. To his credit, he didn't tense or flinch. He didn't have an issue with vampires, but slaughtering sleepers for entertainment or dinner made his blood boil. Her green eyes looked directly into his, yet she didn't try to snare him, but he could sense her trying to send him some kind of message.

He didn't have time to figure out it out as he saw Fang getting ready to leave his seat. Only his superior reflexes and strength kept the pup in his seat. He leaned in close, using an ability unique to Odinsons, he mentally sent Fang a message.

"No matter what happens, we cannot interfere. Stay in your seat and try not to react. It will only feed the vampires' frenzy.

He looked at his brothers, their eyes said as much as his message to Fang had. None of them were pleased and yet they were all trapped in this macabre dance.

Alec removed the hood from the tallest of the captives. Cruel dark eyes sized up the crowd, before the man began to curse and struggle.

The vampire quickly caught his eyes, "Re…"

"NEIN!" A blonde vampire with a thick German accent stood, "The blood tastes better when they struggle, with a heavy dose of fear."

Alec turned his attention back to the struggling man his face becoming a mask of horror as his teeth elongated into razor sharp fangs. The captive scream died as his throat was brutally sliced open, nearly sent Fang to his feet.

Alec repeated the process with the second captive before stepping away and licking the blade clean.

Not one set of eyes looked up at the blood drained from the captives. Every pair of eyes in the room was on them. Viper sat back in his seat willing his posture to relax, then removing his hand from Fang's shoulder.

"Everything all right gentlemen?" the German vampire asked with a feral gleam in his eye. Fresh blood stirred frenzy in vampires and shifters alike. He lifted the dome from the plate in front of him. Large slabs of blue-rare roast beef with all the fixings.

The meat at least should help sate the bloodlust blooming in the shifters unless the vampires intended on making some kind of sport of them. He cut off a chunk of the meat to give it a cursory taste. Perfectly seasoned. Viper didn't taste anything odd so he dug in, thankful the meat would sate his wolf; more thankful Billie wasn't here to witness any of this.

"Just fine, thank you. Delicious meal."

"I'm glad you find it to your liking, not everyone would."

He paused, considering Julian's words. Between that and Velvet's earlier action, he finally understood he wasn't seeing the whole picture. Saving Billie interrupted some important meeting with the big wigs from the council. Viper nodded understanding at the vampire before resuming his meal.

Eventually, servants ladled blood into the vampire's crystal goblets. Fang flinched as the blonde vampire took a long pull from the glass.

"They say the blood of the innocent is tasty. Me," he raised the glass, "I prefer the taste of sin."

Another message with underlying meaning. Viper was relieved to find that the men who died were not innocent. He had no idea if their deeds deserved a death penalty. Perhaps later they'd find out the truth.

The German vampire stood up, throwing his goblet across the room, it shattered in a million pieces.

"What's that supposed to mean? Did you feed us blood from some degenerate you found on the street?"

Lucien stood before Julian had a chance to rise. "You insult your host by insinuating he'd feed a council member trash from the street."

"I demand a fresh supply."

The double doors burst. All heads turned toward the door. Four males wearing biker cuts along with the waitress from the diner strolled in. Fang turned to look at Viper before schooling his face and looking toward his brothers across the table.

Viper examined the waitress, making a mental note of her injuries and bruises, at least the ones he could see.

Then he turned his attention to their host. Julian watched the approach of the group with a bored look in his face. When the group reached the head of the table, he spoke.

"You're late Yannick."

"Got tied up in club business. Some out of town yahoo decided he'd fuck one of my boy's old ladies. We had to knock some heads together."

Viper bit the inside of his lip to keep from laughing, about that time Fang choked on his drink, spitting it out all over the place. The man standing on Yannick's left started looking really hard at Fang.

"Hey, you're the dude that tried to fuck my old lady," the dark-haired man snarled, lunging toward Fang who was out his chair by the time the clearly drunk man headed his direction.

"Enoch enough," Yannick yelled

Too late; the missed lunge meant that Enoch landed in the lap of one of the visiting vampire dignitaries, and of course it had to be the mouthy German. The German vampire grabbed Enoch by the scruff of the neck before throwing him onto the ground one foot on his neck.

"Get your filthy foot off my road captain."

The blonde vampire snarled at Yannick. "Make me, peasant."

Julian stood. "Enough."

He forced enough power into the demand that even the German vampire stilled.

"Yannick, meet Heinrich, one of our visiting council members. Heinrich, Yannick is the President of the Swamp Devils. The motorcycle group who is looking for that little token you want."

"I demand compensation for these insults. I want fresh blood." He lifted his foot off Enoch as he spoke.

"Yannick, since you're late one of yours can feed Heinrich."

Yannick shook with anger pointing to Fang. "He insulted us, and I demand compensation."

"What happens outside these halls are none of my concern. You will wait until my guests leave this property safely. Then, if you can find them, what happens is between the two of you."

Yannick's eyes glowed red and he pushed his power out. Viper felt the wave hit him, but it wasn't directed at him.

Lucien, the tall blonde vampires' eyes bled gold, glowing. He stood up, walked over to Yannick, picked the demon up by the throat, and began squeezing. The power in the room had lesser vampires and shifters on their knees.

"You forget yourself, demon." He shook the demon for good measure before throwing him across the room hard enough to put a dent in the wall.

"Enoch, Heinrich can feed from you."

"No way." Enoch walked over to the waitress, grabbing her by the back of the head. He dragged her in front of Heinrich. "You can have her. Fuck for all I care you can keep her."

Fang stood to his feet. "No. You can feed from me instead, but only if Molly leaves safe with us."

Enoch rushed Fang. Yannick grabbed him by the shoulder long before he reached him.

"We are guests here, there will be no brawling. You gave the woman away. If this is the punk that tried to fuck her in the bathroom, where are his bruises?"

"He must have healed them."

"Go back to the clubhouse. We'll settle this later."

Yannick bowed to Julian. "My apologies to the council."

The demon bowed once again before taking a seat toward the other end of the table.

Heinrich approached Fang looking him over like a piece of meat. Viper didn't like the way this was turning out, but he couldn't get the pup out of this one, not without offering to feed the blonde German vampire himself.

Fang, for his part, stood, still looking below the vampire's eyes when he came in closer. *Good boy.* He never thought to tell the kid not to look a vampire in the eyes, it appears the kid already knew.

"I'll accept the exchange If I get to feed from my favorite spot."

Viper stood up walking to his brother's side. "And what spot would that be Heinrich?"

A feral smile curved up the corners of the vampire's face. "I prefer to feed from the femoral artery."

He looked at Fang who's face remained neutral. When he thought the kid would freak, he didn't.

"That's fine. Molly leaves safe with us."

Chapter 25

Fang

He didn't relish the idea of some bloodsucker biting into his thigh, but there was no way he'd leave a human woman in the hands of a vampire, much less a member of the vampire council. They were rumored to be particularly vicious. He didn't think Molly would survive. Hopefully, he could get her to safety somewhere far away from New Orleans.

"I accept the trade Julian, and this will satisfy my thirst for a fresh supply. All right boy, take off your trousers and sit on the table."

Fuck! He didn't think he'd have to be naked in front of everyone. Not that he had a problem with nudity or his manhood. He didn't like the idea of doing it in front of a crowd of strangers and vampires at that.

"Wait." The calm voice held a lot of power. A ruggedly handsome vampire stood up. With his wavy dark hair and piercing eyes, the man could have played Dracula in a movie. He was Hollywood material.

"Heinrich."

The blonde vampire turned to bow slightly. "Bane, how may I serve you?"

"You can let me have this tasty morsel for myself. I'm sure Julian has other willing vessels."

"That can be easily arranged."

"Fine, but I get to watch."

"I don't want you gawking."

Julian glided forward. "I believe I have the perfect solution, if you will follow me."

Fang sensed his brothers get up from the table, grouping loosely behind him as Julian led the entourage down a few halls, stopping in front of a set of double doors.

"Here you can have all the privacy you desire."

Bane opened the door turning toward him. Fang followed him into the room. Candles flickered to life when they entered the room. He'd never seen such an opulent bedroom. An enormous four-poster bed sat on a platform. Dark, rich wood with intricate carvings adorned with crimson velvet curtains. The black and gold brocade curtains pulled back and tied with crimson silk rope. Crimson velvet covers and a dozen black and gold brocade pillows adorned the bed.

A deep mahogany wardrobe and dressing table sat to one side. The other side of the room contained a crimson fainting couch, at least that's what they called it in that movie.

So, intent in his surroundings he'd lost track of the vampire until he felt him behind him. He resisted the urge to jump out of his skin.

"A little on the gauche side, no?"

"You don't like the decorations?"

Bane's sexy chuckle slid down his spine, going straight to his groin.

"The decor, no. I prefer sleek and modern, like my penthouse in New York."

"You have a penthouse in New York?"

"Yes, I have properties all over the world. A benefit to being long-lived. What I don't have is unjaded innocence."

Bane's lips were a millimeter shy of Fang's ear. "We are most likely being watched. I didn't trust Heinrich with such a tempting morsel."

He couldn't help but shiver. The man was sex on a fucking stick.

"Does it excite you, the chance of us being watched?" Bane's power caressed down his skin like warm breath, making his cock rock hard. He swallowed before blurting out, "I honestly don't know."

That sexy chuckle nearly made him cream his pants like a thirteen-year-old looking at his first nudie magazine.

"What would you like me to do to you?" Bane's tongue flicked the shell of his ear with expertise honed to perfection. He hit the one spot that always made him weak in the knees. Strong arms wrapped around him. Bane smelled of leather, cognac, and power.

"What do you want to do?" *Fuck did I say that out loud?*

"I could tell you all the delightful things I'd like to do. I imagine I could play your body like a cello. Wrapping around you and playing it until it sings. Your body says that you want me. The question, does your mind follow?"

Puzzlement crossed his face before he remembered the altercation over Molly. Words were not his thing. Instead, he bent his knees; leaning more on Bane, he snaked one hand behind the vampire's head, pulling him down into a kiss.

His cock pressed hard against his zipper.

Fang moaned as Bane's tongue tasted the inside of his mouth. Bane tastes like cognac and blood. That excited him even more. Sex and blood were awfully close for shifters and vampires. Eventually, he drew away, the awkward as fuck angle making his neck cramp.

Bane released him, coming to stand beside him. "Come," he said, reaching for Fang's hand. Fang took his hand allowing the vampire to lead him to the bed. Both nervous and excited he nearly stumbled on the second platform step.

Bane pulled him into an embrace as they stood beside the bed. Their hands roaming over each other's bodies.

He slid Bane's jacket over his shoulders, tossing it on the floor before moving to the buttons.

Bane

He was about to give this boy the time of his life all while Heinrich watched, no doubt gnashing his pointy little fangs in envy. Bane allowed Fang to remove his jacket and unbutton his shirt before he picked him up, tossing him on the bed before climbing up beside him. His fangs popped out in excitement. *How long had it been?* Vampires of a certain age didn't pop their fangs like a noob with zero control.

He moved over top of Fang kissing him forcefully, his tongue plundering the young werewolf's mouth. Bane could feel Fang's hard cock pressed against his thigh. His own manhood strained against his Armani trousers. He would show this pup pleasure as he'd never known before.

Bane had little doubt of his skills as a lover, and he intended to use every bit to make this pup scream his name, all while Heinrich watched. Hmm, he'd make sure to tell the German that Fang was off-limits. He wanted Fang from the moment the youth walked into the dining room. He couldn't have been more than two decades old. Sticking it to the German was just the icing on top of the delicious cake he intended to devour.

His hand glided down Fang's body, trailing down the middle of his chest to his lower abdomen, all the while kissing him with raw passion. Bane moved from Fang's lips kissing along his strong jawline before drawing one earlobe into his mouth. Fang moaned bucking his hips causing delicious friction as their groins rubbed together.

"Fuck."

Bane chuckled, releasing the earlobe, he kissed down Fang's neck stopping at the base he flicked his tongue over the sensitive spot before drawing a bit of flesh into his mouth. He bit down, not breaking the skin, but he did allow his fangs to prick the wolf's smooth flesh. Fang groaned out loud trying to buck him off, most likely to gain control.

Bane used his muscular thighs and superior strength to stay in his position while he continued to lick and suck the delicious hard body beneath him.

"Patience."

Fang

He growled, his wolf pacing to the surface. If he didn't bury his cock in something soon, he was going to explode. Usually, when he was with guys they just fucked and left. Bane seemed intent on driving him insane via foreplay. He didn't want to be patient, he wanted to bust a fucking nut.

The vampire moved down to his nipples, licking, and sucking on them before drawing one into his mouth. He bit down; this time hard enough to break the skin. The moment fangs pierced his skin an orgasm ripped through his body. Hot cum spurted all over him, creating a large wet spot in his jeans.

Bane seemed undisturbed about him cumming and continued to suck his nipple enough to pull drops of blood to the surface. He looked down, catching the edge of the vampire's eyes turn into pools of liquid darkness. His pink tongue darted out to lick the drops of blood from around the nipple.

So many new sensations running through his body, he'd nearly forgotten this was all on camera and his brothers were most likely watching along with who knows how many vampires.

The vampire moved to his other nipple. Fang came again when Bane's fangs pierced his skin, only this time he didn't ejaculate. *What the actual fuck?* He didn't even know that was possible.

"How do you keep doing that."

Bane chuckled; the sexy sound made his limp dick start growing hard again.

"It's one of my, shall we say, gifts. I have an orgasmic bite."

"Every time you bite me, I'm going to cum?"

A slow smile turned up the sexy man's face. Damn, that mustache and soul patch made his dick jump.

"Yes, but it won't be the only way I give you orgasms tonight. I'm going to do things to you no one else has ever done. You'll experience pleasure on a new level."

"What do you get out of it?"

"Many things, including my own pleasure. I love the way you moan when you cum. In fact, I'm going to pull down your pants and lick you clean. Sit up," he said moving off him.

He thought for sure he'd be able to flip him, werewolves were supposed to have superior strength and shit, apparently not when up against a vampire.

He sat up quickly, stripping off his shirt before toeing off his boots. Bane moved to unbutton his fly as soon as the last boot left his foot. His jeans quickly joined the rest of his clothes on the bed.

He lay naked on top of the crimson velvet bed. The vampire's dark head was between his legs. He licked off every drop of cum from his skin, before moving down and licking his balls. Bane licked the raphe on his sack. He had no fucking clue that line down the middle of his ball sack was so sensitive.

Fang bit the inside of his lip. Fuck, everything this guy did felt like heaven. He closed his eyes, enjoying the feel of Bane's mouth on his balls. After licking the raphe a few times, the vampire drew his balls into his mouth. Fang felt the razor-sharp tips of Bane's fangs against his balls, but the vampire didn't bite down. He only applied the most delicious amount of pressure. Fang writhed on the bed, twisting the velvet cover in his hands.

Bane started at the base of his shaft licking him like an ice cream cone before he licked the precum off the tip. Wiggling his agile tongue in the opening before he swallowed my whole shaft. At eight and a half inches, he'd never had anyone deep throat him before. The feeling was in-fucking-credible. He found Bane's name spilling from his lips.

He could feel his tight throat muscles wrapped around his rock-hard cock. His chin up against his balls. Bane began moving his head up and down my shaft. Reaching for him, Fang wrapped both hands around the back of his head. Hips bucking of their own volition, meeting his mouth thrust for thrust.

"Fuck Bane."

Bane increased speed. One thumb applied pressure to his taint sending his pleasure shooting through the roof. He cried out as another orgasm rocked his body. *Fuck, fuck, fuck.*

"How the fuck do I keep having orgasms without cumming?" he panted as Bane released his softening cock.

Bane

"Orgasms and ejaculations are not synonymous."

"What are you, a walking dictionary of sex?"

"It would be sad indeed to have been around as long as I have and not know how to please a lover. I'm not done with you yet. We do need lube."

"I have some in my pocket."

Bane watched as Fang moved to get off the bed, he could tell the lad's legs were a bit wobbly. He chuckled quietly, watching that sweet bare ass bent over to pick up his jeans. He retrieved a small, clear plastic bag, bringing it back to the bed he handed it to Bane.

Bane opened the bag upending the contents: a card for the free clinic to get tested, a peppermint, a condom, and a packet of lube.

"Wherever did you find this?"

"They give them out at clubs."

He palmed the lube, sweeping the other contents on to the floor before pulling his young lover back in for a passionate kiss. Their tongues met in an erotic dance; his nipples hardened in anticipation.

Reluctantly he pulled away, "Tell me Fang, are you a top or bottom?"

"Top."

Bane leaned in his lips barely a breath away, erotic energy flowed from him in waves. "So am I."

His very words held erotic power. "Would you be willing to bottom for me?"

Bane was near giddy with anticipation of introducing Fang into a world he'd never known. A new level of pleasure. He watched the play of emotions on the young man's face. Bane had the power to persuade the boy regardless of his actual decision. Only rape in any form wasn't his thing.

Pure pleasure came from consent, regardless of the scene enacted in the bedroom. He had lovers in the past that wanted the helpless, non-consensual experience. Bane went over every detail in a fastidious nature beforehand making sure his lover knew to use the safe word if the scene became too real. Even with consent, it wasn't to his liking.

"Can we stop if I don't like it?"

Bane kissed him this time and for the first time allowed a bit of emotion to mix with his passion. Fang had given him a gift few vampires ever get trust.

"Immediately. Have you used a safe word before?"

"No, not really. What's that?"

"Choose an unusual word, something you wouldn't normally say. If you want to stop, say your safe word."

"Beetlejuice."

"Shall we begin?"

"I want to see you naked."

Bane smiled, unbuttoning, then unzipping the dark trousers, sliding them over his hips as his erection sprang free.

Fang's eyes widened. "Damn."

Emotions once again played on the boy's face; Bane decided to take a slight detour. He stroked his shaft pulling the foreskin back over the mushroom head of his cock.

"Have you ever seen anyone uncut before?"

Fang shook his head. Bane moved closer continuing to manipulate the foreskin. "There are dozens of nerve endings in the foreskin. Touching it adds an extra layer of pleasure for me."

Fang reached out, putting his hand over Bane's shaft. Bane put his hand on top of the wolf's. Showing him how to manipulate the soft skin. The pleasure had him closing his eyes. He swallowed, focusing on showing Fang how to please him.

"Lay face down for me." Bane's eyes bled into black pools void of light as his darker nature came to the surface needing to bury himself inside Fang. He quickly lost patience.

Fang stopped stroking him laying face down on the bed. His head resting on crossed arms. Bane stopped for a moment looking over every inch of the pup. *A tasty morsel indeed.* He'd half expected Heinrich to come bursting through the doors, jealous of the "plunder" he'd stolen from him. The German was a cruel son of a bitch and would have found a way to scar the young man in some permanent fashion.

Beauty such as this should be left unmarred as long as possible. The smooth near hairless muscular skin, nothing short of perfection. Bane moved onto the bed, starting by straddling Fang's ass, his legs bearing the brunt of his weight, he bent down kissing along the back of his lover's neck.

Licks, nips, and kisses along the back of his neck, then down his spine to the triangle where his ass cheeks rounded. Bane moved his body lower with each kiss. He applied pressure to the spot, an often-unknown erogenous spot. Fang's moans met his ears spurring him on, he kissed down his ass cheeks. With one hand he continued to massage Fang's lower back, the other he pressed his thumb into the pup's taint. His fingers playing with his balls.

Slowly, using a little gift he picked up along the way, he moved their bodies down the mattress until his knees rested off the bed. Bane moved from one cheek to the next encouraged by Fang's moans. He wanted the pup to enjoy it as much as he would. Eventually, he spread his ass cheeks licking around the rim. His agile tongue pushing past the tight muscle. Fang's cock jumped the moment his tongue breached the muscle crying out in pleasure.

"Put your ass up in the air and stroke your cock for me, Fang."

The pup hurriedly did as told. Bane added more saliva by spitting on the muscle ring before sliding one finger deep inside Fang. His moans became louder. Bane slid one hand over Fang's stroking the pup's thick cock. He added more saliva and a second finger before breaking open the packet of lube and adding a third finger. He was nearly ten inches and thick.

By the time he pushed the large head of his cock inside Fang, the pup was begging to be fucked. Bane eased his way in slowly relishing every inch as the boy's tight muscle made room for his cock. He completely filled the young pup's tight ass. Pulling out just as slow, Fang cried out when the head of Banes cock hit the p-spot sending an additional wave of pleasure through him.

He could feel the pup's sexual energy growing with each stroke. After several slower deep strokes, he picked up speed. With each stroke, the sexual energy in the room increased. Bane closed his eyes allowing the energy to wash over him giving him added pleasure he fed the energy back into Fang with each thrust creating a near orgasmic state of ecstasy. He'd had lovers become addicted to the feel.

Bane reached down drawing Fang's body up from the bed and Into hIs embrace. Thrusting harder and deeper increasing the pleasure for both of them, his length capable of hitting spots most men couldn't. His own orgasm not far off, he thrust deep one last time, bringing his hand to Fang's throat squeezing it while he bit down on the back of his neck piercing his skin.

The orgasm rocked them both while Bane fed on the sexual energy and the pup's blood. He came deep inside Fang's ass filling him with his seed. Fang came again ejaculating this time shooting his load far enough to hit the headboard of the antique bed.

Chapter 26

Viper

While the scene that played out before him was undoubtedly hot, his attention remained on the vampires, with special attention given to Heinrich. Bane's taking his prize pissed the German vampire off. The tension in the room was palpable as Heinrich watched the screen.

Julian led them to a large room set up like a mini-movie theatre. Cameras from the bedroom Bane and Fang occupied broadcast their every move on a custom made eight-foot by fifteen-foot screen.

Most of the occupants of the room seemed to be enjoying the show. The carnal energy in the room rose to a fevered pitch, taking on a life of its own. He half expected an orgy to break out in the viewing room. Maybe vampires had rules when it came to sex. Honestly, he had no idea.

A surge of energy washed over the room, several of its members moaning along with the couple on the screen. Heinrich stood fury written on his face before Viper could make a move the vampire used hyper-speed. He was out of the room and down the hall in a blink of an eye.

Viper watched on the screen as the doors to the bedroom splintered inward the vampire moving through it. On his way out the door, he watched Bane uncouple from Fang, a blade appearing in his hands as he stood and turned around. The blade sliced cleanly through the German vampire's neck. His body, still moving, nearly collided with Bane's. Heinrich's head falling to the floor.

It took him less than twenty seconds to sprint down the hall, his brothers not far behind. Bane still held the blade in his hand when Viper entered the room.

The vampire regarded him calmly before turning towards the bed to look at Fang.

Fang, for his part, turned around, sitting on the side of the bed, his eyes taking in the situation.

He watched as Bane wiped the blade off on the crimson cover before it disappeared.

"Neat trick."

Bane smiled at him. "Yes rather. I'll tell you about it sometime. I need to address the audience now. It appears there's an opening on the council. We'll talk nominations tomorrow. The show is over.

"Gentlemen, I believe we have some business with Julian and his cohorts. If you'll allow me a few moments to get dressed. I'll have them send someone in to clean up later."

The vampire bent over brushing his lips across Fang's temple, "I'm sorry our moment was so rudely interrupted."

Fang laughed, "To be honest I didn't even notice until it was all over."

If a dead body freaked the pup out, he didn't show it. Maybe he wasn't as green behind the ears as he thought.

Julian, Lucien, and Velvet entered the room shortly after Fang and Bane finished dressing. After a brief exchange, they followed Julian toward the back of the house to a family-style room with modern decor. He and the other brothers took over a sectional.

After everyone settled Julian offered everyone a glass of whiskey and a cigar. Velvet chose a thin cigarillo cutting and lit the tip before speaking. "I think we can all use a good smoke after that amazing performance. I especially liked the ending, oh and the bonus footage will go down in history."

Viper couldn't help but smile at the woman's attitude. The comment eased any remaining tension.

Julian cleared his throat, garnering everyone's attention, "In return for saving the woman, we'd like you to retrieve an object for us. The Swamp Devils hasn't had any luck. With a vacant seat on the council, it must be found."

"What are we looking for?" Ghost asked bluntly

"A vampire relic, l'Arche des Morts."

Viper sucked in his breath, "I thought that was a myth."

"It's very real and somewhere in or around New Orleans. It's also being magickally protected from vampire detection."
"Do you have any leads?"

"Talk to Serena. She will be able to help you get started. I've informed Yannich that there is a truce until your task for us is completed."

"Thanks, should make it easier without having to deal with them as well."

Julian stood, handing Viper a white vellum card with his contact information on it.

"After tonight, it might be best to steer clear of this house. Most did not like Heinrich, but even he had allies."

"Will there be trouble from the council for his death?"

Bane answered, "No. I have over a dozen witnesses, and film that can be slowed down showing Heinrich attack first. I'll walk you to the car. The driver will take you to Serena's."

Viper stood up, happy to get out of the plantation. While he didn't mind vampires, he didn't have the stomach for political bullshit. A black stretch limo waited for them outside. Viper, Ghost, and Elvis climbed in first leaving time for Fang to talk to Bane. The latter slid into the car less than five minutes later with Molly in tow.

The ride to Serena's remained mostly silent. Molly huddled in the corner acting like they were going to eat her. Fang wore the cat that ate the canary smile the whole ride, never saying a word.

Serena answered the door quickly when Elvis knocked. She ushered them in; the house smelled like cinnamon, pecans, and brown sugar.

"Billie is in my room, sleeping. I gave her something that should help restore her energy. I made crack bars and praline pecan butter cookies if anyone wants some. I bake when I'm nervous."

Elvis led Ghost and Fang into the kitchen. He seemed to know his way around.

"Did leaving us with the vampires make you nervous?"

"Yes, because I recognized one of the council member's assistants. I didn't know they were visiting, still, there wasn't another solution. Did they make you pay dearly?"

"They want us to find an object for them, said you might be able to help us."

"Ahh, yes the Swamp Devils were supposed to find that, only I won't deal with demons. They are on their own finding the ark. Let me go get the riddle, as far as I know, it's the only written clue."

She came back a few minutes later, handing him a vellum envelope yellowed with age. He pulled out the paper, unfolding it and scanning its contents.

An original parish of New Orleans. I once had a longer name but now it's been shortened. You'll find me near the world's longest street where a devil tricked an angel.

Overland and under dock,

Once you have tomorrow's dead,
Break apart the hindering block,
Lay it on the argent head.
Count the towers on the crock,
Enter by the moonlight lock,
Terrors full fill every thought,
Count the pure and silent knock.

Viper whistled, "This should be a lot of fun. Any idea what it means?"

She shook her head, "Not my place to unravel the riddle. Do you want to come back and get Billie in the morning?"

"I can carry her if she needs to sleep."

"She does."

Chapter 27

Death

She woke up in a tangle of limbs and blankets, opening her eyes to find Logan laying next to her. He opened his eyes when she tried to move.

"Good morning."

"How did we get back to the house?"

"I carried you. Serena gave you something to help you sleep and replenish your energy."

"I do feel great this morning. I want to rent a Jeep, grab some real food, and visit Marie Laveau's grave before dark."

"We'll need to get something to leave for an offering."

"Rum, silver coins, and flowers."

"How do you know?

"I stayed in the area for a while. I'm going to take a long hot shower."

"Company?"

"If it's you, always."

She did feel amazing this morning. Like a whole new woman, of course, she admitted the man had gotten under her skin. Billie headed to the bathroom, turning on the hot water before grabbing towels. She stripped out of her clothes quickly adjusting the showerhead before stepping in.

Billie stepped into the shower closing her eyes and enjoying the hot water. Cold air hit her skin briefly as Logan opened the curtain long enough to step in behind her.

He slid his arms around her, pulling her flush against his body. She could feel his cock pressing against her.

Fuck if this man didn't have her in perpetual heat. Wildfire spread throughout her body as he cupped her full breasts, working the nipples with his fingers. She arched her back, a small moan escaping her lips.

Billie pushed her ass up against his cock, grinding against him. In response, he positioned it in between her ass cheeks. This time when she ground against him her cheeks slid up and down his shaft.

"Where's the soap?" he growled in her ear.

Billie opened her eyes, spotting the soap on the shower floor in front of her. She bent over to pick it up. Viper took advantage running one finger along her slick folds sending more heat racing through her body. She gave him the liquid soap.

Viper reached around her, adjusting the showerhead to the side, he then poured a generous amount of soap into his hands. He began to soap her body, stroking her breasts, then down her chest; he played with her belly button. His hands slid to her abdomen, slick with soap, his fingers played with the sensitive skin along her pelvic bone before one hand slid down into her curls.

Logan teased her, paying no attention to her slick folds as he washed around them. His hands easing apart her thighs he soaped them up next. He washed her from head to toe, teasing her. Bringing her body to the edge, but not letting her fall over. She whimpered when he turned the shower head back to rinse off the soap while he started on her back. His strong, calloused hands felt amazing on the sensitive skin of her back. When he reached her ass, he took particular care soaping the area, running one finger around her rim. No one had played with her ass before him, it excited her and made her apprehensive at the same time.

"Step forward, baby."

Billie moved forward, allowing the water to slide down her back and wash away all the soap. He dropped to his knees and spread her ass cheeks, his tongue flicking against her tight rim. She moaned loudly as new pleasures rocked her body. Logan's thumb found the tiny bundle of nerves at the apex of her womanhood, rubbing it in circles he slid one long finger inside her wet fold, at the same time his tongue pierced her anal ring.

"Fuck," she cried, her knees nearly buckling.

"Lean up against the wall, baby."

Billie leaned on the shower wall, her arms out bent slightly forward, legs spread as wide as the shower would allow. His fingers and tongue working in unison to fuck her. She closed her eyes again as the hot water and the hotter sensations Logan caused had her shaking and moaning. God, she knew every one of his brothers could hear her, yet when he took her over the edge this time, she didn't hold back screaming his name.

Her legs trembling from the immensity of the orgasm, only it wasn't over. Billie's inner vaginal and anal muscles began to contract at the same time. Her core and clit became ten times more sensitive, each stroke causing so much pleasure it was almost painful. She nearly cried uncle and begged him to stop. He did pause, standing behind she felt the head of his cock against her swollen lips.

When he slid deep inside her, she cried out. Her cries of pleasure increased as he picked up speed, slamming in and out of her dripping wetness. His large hands supported part of her weight as his balls slapped against her.

His moans and grunts join her moans and cries of pleasure in an orgasmic symphony. Logan thrusts, so deep the head of his cock banged against her cervix. Another experience that blurred the line of pain and pleasure.

"That feels so fucking good, Logan. I love that big cock buried deep inside me."

The words slipped out before she could quell them. Her words only spurred him on his thrust increasing to a brutal pace. Sensations began to overwhelm her. Billie thought she saw stars, blacking out for a few seconds. Her senses fully kicked back in when Logan exploded deep inside her setting off another orgasm.

They both slid to the floor, the lukewarm water finally turning cold. Neither had the strength to get up yet. Good sex made you feel weak in the knees. Apparently, great sex caused blackouts and paralysis.

A few minutes later she managed to sit up turning off the shower. Logan stood up behind her helping her to her feet.

"You were beyond amazing, baby." He said kissing behind her ear.

"What did I do beside moan?"

"Are you kidding? Just knowing I pleased you gave me pleasure. Your moans are so fucking hot."

"Really?"

"Yes. We better get dried off and get out of here before we wind up spending the day in bed."

"Not a bad way to spend the day."

"Not bad at all, but we have a new mystery to solve. I'll tell you while we get dressed."

Viper

He explained everything that happened after the graveyard, glossing over the bedroom scene.

"So, we have the waitress, Molly, and we're supposed to retrieve some artifact for the vampires?"

"Yes."

"I'm sorry."

"About what?"

"I've cost you something else. Money for Cayum and now this."

"Cayum is a lowlife, pond-sucking scuzzball that needs to be gutted. Never feel sorry for getting away from him or Odin's own stepping in. You're family now, Death."

He crossed the room taking her in his arms and kissing her. The kiss was soft, sweet, and gentle. His wolf may not have claimed her as a mate, but he loved her, nonetheless.

"I love you, Billie Cameron. Together we'll find the artifact, clearing our debts to the vampires, and we'll unlock the puzzle in our brains."

"I love you, Logan. I have since you picked me up out of the dirt. I've never been in love before. To be honest, it scares the hell out of me."

He kissed her again, this time pouring his heart into the kiss. Logan began to undress his love; he would show her how much he loved her.

Ghost and Fang waited for them downstairs.

"Where are Elvis and Molly?"

"Elvis took her to the airport. He's putting her on a plane to Tennessee. That's where her family is. Mother found one of the brothers in the area, and he'll keep an eye out on her," Ghost answered.

"Billie wants to rent a cage before we do our errands. We'll need to call a cab so we can get the bikes."

"Already taken care of," Fang said with a grin.

"How did you manage that?"

"I didn't. Bane did. The bikes were in the garage this morning with a note."

"Looks like someone made an impression."

Fang gave him a cocky grin.

"Ghost and I are going to head down to the public archives to see if we can figure out the first part of the riddle."

"Good plan. Billie and I will hit the graveyard."

"What do you plan on doing there?" Ghost asked.

"We're going to leave an offering for Marie."

"I've done it before," Billie chimed in. "I called the rental place; they'll be dropping off a Jeep in the next hour."

Elvis returned, just in time to take with Ghost and Fang. The Jeep arrived shortly after his brothers left.

He climbed in the driver's seat while Billie unfolded the map, she asked the rental company to include, quickly finding the way to the graveyard.

"We'll pass a few places on the way to get supplies."

An hour later they arrived at the gates of St. Louis Cemetery No. 1. Viper stretched out his senses. He didn't detect any ghouls, though the chance of them being around in daytime was slim to none. The amount they ran into last night wasn't normal, and he wanted to be extra careful after last night.

He let Billie lead the way while he continued to scan the area. In no time they arrived at the grave. Billie went first practicing the ritual before making her wish and placing both silver coins and rum on the grave. Viper followed suit, adding a silent prayer to Odin to get the Voodoo Queen's attention.

May ravens on wing carry our message to the spirit world.

Chapter 28

Billie

They walked out of the cemetery, heading to the Jeep. After opening the car door, she spotted a bit of white from the corner of her eyes. Upon investigation she found it to be a business card stuck under the wheel of the truck. Green foil letters advertised the Absinthe Lounge in the French Quarter.

"What did you find?"

"A card for a lounge in the French Quarter."

"I could use some food."

"I'll drive, I know the way."

"Fine by me."

It took five minutes to arrive at their destination. Billie didn't have any trouble finding a parking spot. She spotted a sign in the rearview mirror. Bold black letters proclaimed the shop's name: The Prophecy.

"Babe, turn around."

Logan turned around looking across the street behind them. He whistled.

"Looks like my stomach can wait."

He took her hand leading them across the street. A warm wave of energy greeted them as they crossed the threshold. The shop contained stones, dried herbs, and various other magickal accouterments. Soft instrumental music played in the background. Billie noticed an altar with rum, silver, and tobacco moments before a man appeared not far from them.

She was certain he wasn't there a few moments ago. Tall, on the thinner side, his dark hair was done in twists, unblemished mahogany skin, and brilliant green eyes. A generous smile showed even white teeth.

"Welcome to The Prophecy, I'm Lance Laveau. How can I help you?

"Laveau as in Marie?

His smile widened. "Indeed, I'm one of her grandchildren. How may I be of service?"

Logan stepped up, offering his hand. "My name is Logan Haagan. An acquaintance of mine said I could find a seer, related to Marie with eyes like water."

"That could be a fair lot in this area. We have some muddy waters."

"I got the distinct feeling the seer we're looking for would have blue eyes."

"That does make a difference. You'll be wanting my sister, Merci."

"Great," Billie said excitedly. "Where can we find her?"

A frown marred Lance's handsome face. "I wish I knew. We have not seen her for some weeks now."

"Can you not use magick to locate her?" Billie inquired.

"I can beseech the loa on your behalf. Perhaps they will answer for you."

"Please, do so," Logan added.

She watched as Lance pulled a leather-bound calendar looking at the dates. "I have two nights from now open, will that work?"

"Is there any way you can do it sooner?"

"Come with me."

Billie looked at Logan before following Lance. He led them to a side room. The small dark room barely fit the three of them. A black cloth covered table sat in the middle of the room. Lance indicated Billie and Logan sit one side while he took a seat on the other.

"Let me see your hands?"

Both Billie and Logan held their hands' palms up for his inspection. He looked at Logan's first.

"The hands of a warrior, and one of Odin's own." Lance dropped Logan's hand and took one of hers into his. He traced the lines in her hand with the tip of his finger.

"You're a twin."

"I am?"

"You don't know?"

"No."

"How is that possible?"

"I have no family, at least none that I can remember."

"Who raised you?"

"The streets."

It was like a light went off in Lance's head. "I'll be right back. I need to lock up and put up the closed sign."

Lance came back into the room. "I will do the ceremony alone if the two of you will wait up here. There's a small kitchen in the back if you get hungry; this could take a while.

Two hours later Lance returned unkempt a look of exhaustion on his face.

"I'm afraid all I have is more riddles. Images actually. A skull and crossbones, a white house and a road made of water."

"Thanks," Logan replied, "it's more information than we had."

"Tell me, are you seeking Merci because of the prophecy?"

"Prophecy?" She and Logan asked nearly in unison.

"Let me catch your eyes. Ladies first."

"Like a vampire?" Her hands trembled slightly, and she reached for Logan's hand.

"Not unlike one, yet different. I will have no control over you. My gift allows me to see things. Things even your mind hides from you."

"What will you see?"

"Everything."

"It's all right baby, I'll be right here with you."

She swallowed and nodded her head bringing her eyes to meet Lance's. His green eyes filled with kindness. Billie relaxed while leaves swirled around her vision. Suddenly she sensed another presence in her mind. It triggered a memory.

Lance

The moment he breached her last defense a gruesome scene immediately played out.

Billie strapped to a St. Andrew's cross. Surrounded by five vampires, one at each point of the cross and one behind her, biting her neck. He heard masculine laughter in the background.

"This is what you get for disobeying me, Billie. I told you to take out your opponent."

She struggled to talk in between screams of terror. "I won. I broke her and she'll never fight again. Please, Cayum, please make it stop."

"But you didn't kill her, did you?"

"No," she sobbed.

He withdrew from the rest of the memory. It's not what he's looking for. Poor girl. Lance could only imagine the atrocities she endured under the Dark Fae's hand. He shivered. Lance was well acquainted with Cayum, having seen what he'd done firsthand on numerous occasions. After his contract with Cayum ended, he walked away and never looked back. Two of the longest years of his life.

He pushed deeper into her mind.

A toddler dirty, cold, and poorly dressed hiding behind a dumpster. A fiend searching the alley for her. When the fiend came within three feet of the girl, she melted into the background, completely disappearing from view.

A bit too far back. How did a two-year-old wind up on the streets and what horrors had this poor girl seen? Though his age appeared to be late twenties, Lance was over one hundred and fifty years old. His mother, Marie-Angelie Paris, was Marie's eldest daughter. One rumored to have died at the age of seven. She gave birth to Lance at the age of sixteen. His sister, Merci, was born a decade after his birth. He raised that girl as much as his mother did. He sent up a prayer to the ancestors to watch over his little sister.

Fast forward a few years; Billie must be around eight. He found the girl once again hunkered behind an alley.

A group of teenage boys searched the alleyway. "We know you're here somewhere. You might as well come out."

Lance took time to tune into Billie's emotions. To his surprise, she wasn't scared. He found her plotting how to take the boys out, or the best way to take them out. Her only concern, the number of them. She had nowhere to hide and didn't know how to make her hiding ability work.

Rather than waiting until she was cornered, she kept to the shadows, moving away from the garbage bin where the boys were headed and back down the alley. While she didn't think she would make it out of the alley without being spotted; she wanted to get out of the corner.

Billie made it more than halfway to the street before shouts went up. One of the boys spotted her. Looking around, she quickly grabbed a dented trash can lid and hefty looking stick that was most likely a part of some tool. She took the first three by complete surprise

After that, the boys regrouped and came at her from different directions. She managed to stop them from completely surrounding her, yet it was clear she was outnumbered. The street was still too far to run, and she was quickly becoming boxed in despite her best efforts when a howl split the air.

A massive wolf, bigger than the pony she'd seen at the carnival, appeared behind the boys coming out of the darkness. Teeth bared, saliva dripping from its jaws. Billie knew she should be just as terrified as the boys. One by one they ran past her as the wolf advanced.

Once the boys left, the wolf began to shift into a man. She watched him grow, up and up, until he towered over her. A barrel-chested wall of muscle, Billie looked up to see his face.

Suddenly he ran into a blank spot. Energy tried to push him out of Billie's mind. Lance called upon his magickal might and managed to stay in her mind. He gently probed the block, looking for a crack in the essence of the spell that kept her memories blocked. He went slowly, methodically searching until he spotted a small chink in the block. Lance sent a small stream of energy through the tiny pinhole. Like water, the energy slowly made the hole bigger. As soon as the hole was large enough, he slipped through.

A fully clothed Viper, complete with OWMC vest and patch, stood over the little girl. He bent down to her level. It was then that Lance noticed the cross necklace around the girl's neck. Magick energy emanated from it.

Lance viewed the remainder of the memory contained in the blocked section before withdrawing from her mind.

He took a deep breath pulling out slowly out of Billie's mind. He smiled. "How do you feel?"

"Weird, but all right."

"Viper I'd like to delve into your mind first, then I'll answer any questions you have."

The wolf shifter nodded in agreement.

Lance dove into the shifter's mind, heading straight for the same time frame he encountered the block in Billie's mind. He found the same type of magickal block in place.

This time as he searched, he found a hole. Just big enough for his conscience to slip through. As he viewed the same scenes from Viper's point of view, he felt the presence of wolf energy. Viper's wolf "stood" beside him, viewing the memories that contained Billie.

Once the wolf had seen enough, he took off, bashing a bigger hole in the block on his way out. Viper's energy shifted and it became impossible for Lance to stay in any longer.

Chapter 29

Viper

He didn't need Lance to tell him what he found; his wolf delivered the news to him with such swiftness, it felt like someone hit him between the eyes with a 2 x 4.

MATE! roared through his brain slamming his heart against his chest.

Memories of the street urchin he taught to fight flooded back into his mind. He tried to get her to come with him, to stay in a home, but she was too afraid.

Viper was called away on a mission and had to leave. When he returned a few weeks later, she was gone.

"Easy wolf, she does not yet remember. It will take Merci's special abilities to remove the blocks," Lance said gently.

Billie looked at him with confusion painted across her face. Her green eyes asked a million questions.

"Lance, can you explain?"

The man smiled, "Of course. Billie, I wanted to enter Viper's mind right after yours to see if you had the same block put in place."

"What do you mean by block?"

"Someone has placed a magickal barrier around part of your memories, Viper's as well. Do you remember the fight in the alley when you were around eight?"

Billie nodded her head.

"Do you remember the wolf?"

"Yes, a big wolf came and chased them all off, but he didn't hurt me."

Viper took both of Billie's hands in his, turning her so they faced each other. "I was the wolf. We spent a few weeks together after that. I trained you to fight but you refused to let me take you someplace safe. To a home or a family."

"I don't remember any of that. Why do you remember?"

"My wolf. Somehow while Lance was probing around inside my head, the wolf broke through the block."

Billie turned to face Lance. "You think Merci will be able to remove mine?"

"Yes, but there is more. I believe your part of a prophecy. I'll share with you what I know. Merci has the rest of it."

An angel sent to avenge the wrongs will find love in the arms of a wolf.

When two worlds collide, a child will sacrifice it all to awaken the father of fangs.

"You think the first line is about us? I'm no angel."

"I think you are much more than you realize. Having your memories back will help, but I believe Merci is the key to finding your true self."

Viper rubbed his thumb on the back of Billie's hand. "We got this."

She looked at him unshed tears brimming in her eyes, "You remember?"

"Yes." He wanted to add 'and that's not all.' Viper would claim her as his mate soon enough.

"Thank you, Lance, for all your help." Viper pulled out several bills from his wallet and paid the man for his services.

"Let's go find the brothers and see if they made any headway on the riddle. We have more information we can add to it."

"One more thing before you go," Lance added. "Billie's necklace is more than it seems. I'm not an expert on magickal items, but I believe it will help reveal her true identity."
"Thanks again. We'll look into the necklace as well."

Viper pulled out his phone sending a quick text to his brothers. "Let's grab some food we can take back. We can shop for groceries later."

"We'll need plates and silverware."

"The pup took care of that this morning while we were sleeping."

They sat around the table enjoying the food and each other's company. Billie gave as good as she got, cutting up and joking with the brothers. He longed to tell her she was his one true mate but now was not the time. After the meal, they went over the information each had found.

Fang handed Billie the list of parishes he found earlier since she spent time living in the area. She and Elvis had the best chance of recognizing the clues.

"Wait! I think I know where this is. White House, I bet that's E.D. White's house in Thibodaux. Hey, I think they also have some kind of preserve for Jean Lafitte."

"The skull and crossbones, Lance saw." Viper added.,

"Yes, I think so, plus Bayou Lafourche is sometimes referred to as the longest Main Street in the world. It runs in between two highways for over a hundred miles."

Elvis whistled, "That's a lot of ground to cover."

"But the clues seem to point us to Thibodaux, and I think that Lafitte's park is less than forty square miles. It's a lot, but better."

"Who's up for a road trip?" Viper asked.

"You know it," Fang said.

"Count me in, brother," Ghost added.

"Mmm, time to suck some tasty butts," Elvis said with a grin.

Fang poked Elvis as he said, "Dude! There's a lady in the house."

Billie laughed, "I've heard worse in the ring, but I appreciate the thought."

Elvis bust out laughing, "No, no. I'm talking about mudbugs, crawfish, crawdads, Louisiana lobster."

Viper laughed along with everyone else.

"It's supposed to be suck the head and squeeze the butts," Billie added, still laughing.

"Let's pack and meet back in fifteen."

He hurried up the stairs to the bedroom he and Billie shared, pulling out both of their bags. Billie not far behind him went to the bathroom and gathered both of their things, placing them in separate bags before adding them to their duffels.

"I'll call the rental company and have them pick up the car. I'll tell them they can keep the week's rental fee. I think that should get them here quickly."

"Good plan, babe. I'll finish packing while you talk to the car place."

He watched her step out on their small balcony, cell phone to her ear. Viper packed his clothes first, then took more time to pack hers. Each item held a memory of them together. He felt like a newborn pup around her. Raging hormones, awkward conversations, and finding his first true love.

He'd been in love before, even had a few long-term relationships. Well, long term in sleeper years. One lasted a quarter of a century. This was different, now the block had been breached, he knew why. Billie is his mate.

Viper went back to packing Billie's gear. He didn't have time to gather wool.

Chapter 30

Billie

They rode into town on their bikes, Billie the only one without a cut. She wondered if they would admit non-wolf members. She already felt like a part of their family. That's what most MCs became, families. Even the outlaw groups still had each other's backs.

The brothers decided to let Billie lead the way, she followed her nose. She had an acute sense of smell. Not wolf acute, but still damn good. Billie stopped in front of a place called Boo's. According to the signs, it's famous for gator gumbo and mudbug stew.

A band played lively zydeco music. They usually didn't start live music until after dark. It was still early evening. The festive atmosphere reminded her of the time she spent in the area. She briefly wondered if she would have stuck around had Cayum not found her.

"I'll go see how long the wait is," Fang said as he headed toward the door.

He came back a few minutes later. "It's going to be at least forty-five minutes."

"I'll go book some rooms, any suggestions?" Logan asked.

"I think I know a place, bro," Elvis claimed.

Logan pulled Billie into his arms for a quick kiss. "We won't be long. Try and keep the pup out of trouble."

Billie laughed, laying her head on his shoulder as she drank in his warmth. She could get used to this. Him being around. Having a family. A place where she belonged. Billie watched as Logan and Elvis rode off.

Ghost placed a hand on her shoulder, "I'll go get us a couple of brews."

"Thanks, Ghost."

He smiled, showing perfect white teeth and dimples. She could see them beneath the beard. "That's what family's for."

A lone tear slid down her face. She quickly wiped it away as Ghost headed inside.

"Hey, you, all right?" Fang asked softly.

"I've never had a family before.

The pup surprised her by pulling her into a tight hug. "Me either."

They were the same height flat-footed and in their thick-soled, ass-kicker boots.

"I'm pretty impressed by the way you stepped up to save Molly. I think we got off on the wrong foot."

"Nah, I was a jerk. I fucked up and after Viper explained everything to me, I wanted to make up for it."

He smiled widely. "Besides, I got the best sex of my life out of it. I'm fairly certain Bane has spent most of his centuries learning about sex. I mean damn."

Billie laughed. "I'm glad you enjoyed yourself."

"Enjoyed hell and learned some things. Now I need a sweet piece of pussy to make my night better."

She laughed, shaking her head. "Be careful, these Cajun boys are pretty possessive of their women, and protective of their daughters."

"Hmm, maybe I should run my choice by you."

"Your best bet is a divorcee, preferably one not dating someone else or with a crazy ex."

"I'm supposed to find all this out in one night?"

"It's called conversation, Sherlock. Pay attention to more than her tits and ass. Be charming, ask questions, and listen."
"Fuck, that's a lot of work."

"How did you find girls before?"

He shrugged his shoulders. "Sex is easy to find. Wham, bam, you move on, and that's it."

Ghost came back with three long necks.

"It's different when you have a family, pup. Don't get me wrong, there's always plenty of pussy around but when you're on a mission you put that aside. Or, at the very least make sure it's not going to cause issues."

Billie took a long pull from the cold beer listening to the brothers banter back and forth.

"Odin, party of five", came over the loudspeakers, causing her to nearly spit her beer out. Ghost laughed, clapping his brother on the back. "Good choice."

"And good timing," Logan added as he and Elvis walked up to them, sliding his arm around Billie.

She smiled tilting her head up to meet his kiss. It was sweet, soft, and way too fast, but they were in public. Billie slid her arm around his waist as they walked into Boo's.

Viper

They were seated at a six top far enough away from the band they could talk, but close enough to enjoy the music and the energy it made. He sat on one end with Billie to his left and Elvis on her other side. The two chatted about what they planned on ordering from the menu.

He couldn't help but smile watching his mate talk animatedly to his brother. The two chattering on and off in French, the secondary language of the area. She'd come alive in the last few days. Damn, he'd known her for less than a week. Not counting his recently recovered memory. One that made him realize he still knew extraordinarily little about the woman he loved. Whatever her past, it didn't matter. They'd face it together.

Viper slid his arm behind Billie, resting it comfortably on the back of her chair. He enjoyed being close to her. Honestly, the last couple of days with her and his brothers had been some of the best in his long life.

A pretty waitress with her flaming red hair in two braids and the name tag that read 'Ruby Mae' bounced up to the table. A light dusting of freckles only added to the girl's appeal. She put on her best smile, meeting everyone's eyes with the same level of enthusiasm.

Her Cajun accent was thick. "Hi y'all, my name is Ruby Mae. I'll be taking care of you this evening."

She handed out the menus as she spoke. "What can I get you to drink?"

Viper pointed to the bottles of beer. "We'll take another round of these and keep them coming."

"We'll do, chér."

"Oh, the waitress is flirting with your man, Death. What are you going to do about it?"

Billie laughed, "I'm going to give her a big tip if she keeps bringing us cold brew and hot food. What are you going to do about it?"

Fang smiled, showing off that kilowatt smile that would undoubtedly get them into more trouble. Most likely sooner rather than later. Though he didn't expect the pup would repeat the mistake he made earlier.

Ruby Mae came back to the table a few minutes later. "Would you like to start with appetizers?"

"Too bad it's not soft-shell season, Logan. You'd love their parmesan soft shell crabs."

From his vantage point, he could see both Billie and Ruby's faces. Billie had a soft, faraway look, like a good memory surfaced. Ruby Mae wrinkled her nose like something was niggling at her memory.

"You'll have to visit us again come March. We have blazin' shrimp tonight. They're about three times the size of the popcorn. The boys had a good run and sold us the extra."

"Babe do you want to order for everyone?"

"Yes! We'll take two orders of those, fried green tomatoes, frogs' legs, crab fingers, two sampler platters, and two crawfish bread."

Ruby Mae smiled, "I like the way y'all eat. Let me put these in, grab you another round, and then I'll get your dinner order."

"Either a lot of big eaters in this area…" Viper started.

"Or a lot of sups," Ghost finished.

"Which means we are probably on someone's turf right now," Elvis added.

"Let me think for a minute," Billie said.

She put her thumb to her mouth chewing on the nail while she thought. Her nails must grow fast; he'd never noticed them "chewed down".

"Gators. I don't remember their name."

"Do you remember their leader's name?" he asked her softly.

"It starts with an H, I think. Umm, Hank, Herbert."

"It's Hervé. Hervé Laffitte is who you want to let know you're in town and for how long. He'll be in shortly for dinner." Ruby Mae said, sitting down fresh beers as she loaded the empty bottles on a tray sitting it at the table's empty spot before taking out her order pad and pen.

"I'm ready if you are. Your appetizers should be out in about five minutes. We have an extra cook on busy nights."

"Is that why the larger order didn't seem odd?"

She smiled. "You could have had appetizers for dinner, but your energy gave you away. Out here the further into the swamp the more likely you are to find otherkin. All kinds of things that go bump in the dark out here."

Her smile slipped for a brief second before it slipped back into place, but the darkness lingered in her eyes. "What can I get you?"

Billie listed off a dozen or more dishes from gumbo to roast duck and more frog legs. Said she had a feeling they'd go over big.

Chapter 31

Billie

The moment Hervé walked in, she remembered him. Only ten years turned him from a gangly youth into a full-blown man. His swimmers build more linebacker now. The hair he kept buzzed nearly reached his shoulders in dark waves. Dark brown eyes spotted the newcomers immediately; it took him until he reached the table to recognize her.

"Billie is that you, chér? I haven't seen you in a coon's age."

She stood up as he approached the back of her chair. He embraced her in a quick hug.

"Ooo wee girl, you're nigh as tall as I am. What brings you and your friends here?"

"Why don't you set down, Hervé? We just ordered. Ruby Mae should be back with another round."

Elvis stood up offering the man his chair. He took it with a thank you and a wink.

"My friends and I are on vacation." The lie rolled easily off her tongue as she reached for Logan's hand. "I wanted to show my boyfriend some of my old stomping grounds."

"And all wolves travel in a pack?"

She smiled. "Something like that, yes."

By that time Ruby Mae arrived with another round, her eyes widened a little when she spotted Hervé sitting at the table. She bowed her head briefly in submission. "Good evening Mr. Laffitte, you're early today."

He smiled. "I heard we had a few visitors in town. Imagine my surprise when one of them turns out to be Billie Cameron, our long-lost friend."

The waitress's eyes once again widened in surprise. "I thought I recognized you. You probably don't remember me; we only met a few weeks before that slick-talking devil came taking you away."

"Thankfully, that's all behind me. I do remember you. You used to sneak me food out of the orphanage."

"That's right." Ruby Mae smiled. "I'll go get your usual, Mr. Lafitte and put in your dinner order."

"Thank you, Ruby Mae."

Hervé turned his chair toward Billie leaning in closer. "I get the feeling; you're not giving me the whole truth. Since we're old friends and I know dat you spent a decade with that Dark Fae Capo, I'm going to let it slide for now. There will be a time you'll need to trust me. Make sure you don't do anything that would break my trust in you."

Billie nodded her head. "This is Viper, Ghost, Fang, and Elvis."

"Elvis, thanks for the seat. Can you dance like him?"

"You bet," Elvis replied smiling. Billie could have sworn she heard someone sigh when her brother turned on his best smile. He had charisma for days.

After Ruby Mae dropped off a double scotch on the rocks the boys launched into small talk. The tension in the atmosphere eased.

As the band started another lively number, the gator shifter stood suddenly reaching for her hand. "You do remember how to dance, don't you?"

She laughed. "I do. I think. Guess we'll find out."

Viper

He watched his mate get led onto the dance floor by the gator shifter. Hervé doing his best to feel them out and passing it off as small talk. Not a bad plan. They had nothing to hide, well almost nothing. Viper didn't know who to trust outside of his group. Now it was clear that someone in the preternatural world didn't want him and Billie together. Whoever they were, they had enough money and power to place a block inside one of Odin's own. Not an easy task.

Ruby Mae came back, followed by three other servers who placed large laden trays on stands before leaving. She quickly placed the food on the table adding several more dishes in front of the gator's seat.

He stopped her. "What can you tell me about Hervé?"

She shook her head. "What do you want to know? He's a great boss. Own's Boo's and several other places in town."

He decided to let it drop. They were in a public, not the best place to get potentially sensitive information.

"Good to know, say what do you think of the Dansereau House?"

"It's a great place to stay. I love the Rose Suite. It's my favorite. Are you staying there?"

"Booked the last two suites."

"You'll love the place."

Hervé and Billie returned from their dance, his mate smiling and laughing.

"What place is that chér?"

"Billie is staying at the Dansereau House."

"Really?" Billie exclaimed. "I always wanted to stay at that place."

Viper pulled her in for a quick kiss. "Well, now you are."

"These smells delicious. Let's dig in."

"Ladies first, my love."

She smiled filling her place she even grabbed some of the gator's escargot.

"Always thieving my food."

"Hey, you said you'd always share."

Hervé ruffled Billie's hair. "Bottomless pit of a kid."

"Better eat before I go back for seconds."

"Ha, I can order more."

Billie looked up noticing that Ruby Mae and several other people were staring at them.

"Why's everyone looking at us?"

"'Cause I'm a mean ol' gator playing like a cub."

"If you say so. Frog legs?"

They spent much of the next two hours, eating, drinking, and listening to music. Hervé insisted on buying them all dinner, so Viper left a huge tip for Ruby Mae. After the short ride to Dansereau's House, he grabbed both his and Billie's bags leading them to their suite.

He watched her as he opened the double doors. Billie's face lit up as she stepped in the large suite, taking in the king-sized bed, dining room table, loveseat, and chair. She gasped when she saw the stained-glass door. Crossing the room, she opened the door to find a large bathroom; complete with a whirlpool tub big enough to fit both of them. Once inside the bathroom, a set of double glass doors led to a balcony.

Billie turned, throwing her arms around Viper's neck. "I love it."

Chapter 32

Death

They spent the next week searching for clues, before heading to Boo's for dinner and drinks. Ruby Mae even hung out with them on her days off. It made her miss Ava; she wished the girl could come be with them. She'd bring her along when she and Logan came back during soft crab season.

Tonight, she had a date with Logan. Just the two of them. The brothers were going to hit a bunch of dive bars. They were supposedly looking for clues, but Billie knew at least two of them wanted to get laid. Logan was out with the boys right now giving her some time to get ready.

She finished drying off when a knock sounded at the door. Wrapping the towel around her body she headed for the door.

"Who is it?"

"Ruby Mae."

Billie opened the door. "Hey girl, I wasn't expecting you, come in."

She held up several bags. "I know you have a hot date with that hunky wolf, and you promised to let me give you a makeover. I don't care how many years ago. A promise is a promise."

She laughed. "All right. I give. You can do a makeover."

"You sit back and relax. I have a cosmetology license; I'm working at Boo's to save up enough to open my own salon."

"Why don't you work in a salon until you can open your own?"

"I tried that, but it didn't work out. Plus, I make bank on weekend nights at Boo's."

"Do you like working for Hervé?"

"He's a fair man, just never cross him. He's vicious, then he has to be to keep a rule on some of these bayou rats. I think you should ask him for help. Tell him what you're looking for."

"How do you know we're looking for something?"

"Not much happens in the area that Hervé doesn't find out about. He asked me if I knew anything. I don't and that's what I told him."

"I'll talk to Logan and see what he thinks."

Ruby Mae spent the next two and a half hours doing Billie's hair, nails, and makeup. She'd never had long nails before. Ruby painted them black with a single white sigil on each nail. They were pointed, resembling shining black claws. Each one of her fingers had at least one silver ring, some had more. A few had a small moonstone in them, while others had onyx, others still were plain bands. The rings were the only jewelry she wore, save the small gold cross around her neck. She'd had the necklace for as long as she could remember.

"You ready to look?"

"Yes!"

Billie turned around, gasping at her appearance. She wore an off the shoulder long-sleeved, black tee with a hand-painted tiger's head in hues of blue and purple. Over the shirt, she wore a bolero style leather jacket with cut out sleeves. Her jeans were faded blue denim on top with black suede that resembled chaps. White roses and vines were embroidered on the suede. Billie's hair lay in soft waves down past her shoulders to the middle of her back.

The makeup Ruby Mae used picked up the green in her hazel eyes. Her lips were a deep shade of red, almost burgundy.

"Chér, you look amazing. You best steer clear of Boo's."

"Why?"

"Because Hervé may stop seeing you as a little sister and decide to give your beau some competition. He loves competition."

"I'll keep that in mind. I have no idea where we're going."

"No matter, you will be the belle of the ball, wherever you go." Billie hugged her friend tightly. "Thank you."

Viper

When Billie came down the stairs with Ruby Mae you could have blown him over with a straw. His jaw damn near dropped to the floor.

"Odin's damn you look good enough to eat."

She smiled, her eyes sparkling with mischief, "I'll break out the little red riding hood outfit later."

"Damn baby, damn, damn, damn." He crossed the room taking her in his arms before kissing her fiercely. He didn't give a damn if he wound up with lipstick all over his face. When the kiss ended, he kept her in his arms, his cock trying to burst from his jeans.

"Are we going to make it to dinner?"

He kissed her again softly. "Yes."

They rode on his bike, Billie's arms wrapped around him. She didn't even complain the helmet would mess up her hair. He drove them to the outskirts of town to a small Italian restaurant named La Bella Cucina. Hervé recommended it when he asked about a romantic place to take Billie. The gator king even called ahead and made reservations.

The hostess led them to a small table in a quiet corner not far from the fireplace. Soft Italian music played in the background.

After looking at the menu, they both decided on spaghetti and meatballs.

"I love Italian food."

"I'm glad I took Hervé's advice then."

"You two seem to be getting along well. Ruby Mae suggested we confide in him. She said he already knows we're searching for something."

"I'll talk it over with the brothers. It's a sound idea. He knows the area better than any of us and we are running in circles at this point."

The waiter brought their food, the meatballs were the size of baseballs. They both dug in with gusto and when nearly all the food was gone, Billie suggested the reenact Lady and the Tramp. They shared the final bite, kissing when the two ends met in the middle.

Just a sweet kiss from her sent fire running through his veins. He couldn't get enough of her. He pulled her from the chair onto his lap kissing her thoroughly until they were both gasping for breath. His hard cock strained against his jeans. Viper could feel her heat through her jean-clad core.

Gently he picked her up from his lap sitting her in the chair long enough to pull out his wallet and threw several bills on the table.

"Ready?"

"Yes."

The ride back to the Dansereau House was nothing short of torture. He needed to be inside her. His wolf pushed him for days to claim her. Tonight, he would claim her as his mate. Once they were inside the house, he swept Billie off her feet carrying her up the two flights of stairs to their third-floor suite. The only other suite on the floor was a family suite occupied by the brothers.

He deposited her on the bed before returning to close and lock the double doors. Billie stood to meet him when he came back. With her high heeled boots on, she was nearly his height. It was so fucking hot.

Viper looked into his mate's eyes. "Babe, when my wolf broke through the block, I realized that you're more than the love of my life; you're my mate. I want to mark you tonight."

"Yes."

"You understand what that means?"

"Yes, one of my trainers is a wolf. She told me about her mark once when we were sparring. My answer is yes."

He didn't know if his heart or his dick would burst first. Crude, maybe, but he was an animal after all. Viper's smile bordered on feral when he took her lips again.

"I don't have a lot of restraint tonight; my wolf is close."

She smiled at him. "Let's see who can undress the fastest." Immediately she started shucking her clothes, kicking off the ankle boots without unlacing them. He watched as she tossed her leather jacket on the floor, her shirt quickly following. When she took her bra off, his mouth watered. *Those tits.* He loved her tits. They fit perfectly in his large hands. Her taught rosy nipples stood at attention begging for his mouth. He peeled his shirt off before staring at his love again.

Kicking off his boots he watched her unbutton the jeans. His jaw dropped when he saw she had no panties on, and what's more, she shaved. A neat landing strip beckoned him.

Viper nearly ripped his jeans off when she stood before him completely nude. His voice a husky growl, "Bed!" His alpha power flowed from him with the word. Billie moved forward two steps from compulsion before she stopped, glared at him, then launched her body across the room, colliding with his. Her long legs wrapped around his waist. Her mouth savaged his mouth. He returned the savage kiss as they toppled onto the bed.

She rode him down to the bed. Pulling her lips away. "No alpha shit in the bedroom unless we talk about it first."

"Oh yeah?" he said as he flipped her. His lips found the fluttering pulse in her neck he bit down hard but didn't break the skin. "I thought you liked this alpha shit."

She moaned, "I do. Just not the command."

Viper blushed. "I didn't intend to do that. My wolf is anxious and a bit unruly."

"Are you saying you can't control your wolf?" One eyebrow quirked and her eyes danced with mischief.

"I'm saying that you make me lose control."

"Oh," she said as she flipped him onto his back again.

"Odin's damn, woman, I lose all sense around you."

"Good," she said softly, placing a soft kiss on his lips before laying her head on his chest. "Now, make me your mate."

He growled; she didn't have to ask twice. Instead of flipping her, he drew her head up for a sensual kiss. His tongue slowly traced her lips before he parted them. He took his time tasting her while their hands roamed each other's bodies.

Viper reluctantly pulled his lips from hers. He kissed up her jaw starting by her chin. When he reached her ear, he drew the lobe into his mouth gently grazing his teeth along the lobe as he sucked.

Billie moaned arching her back against him. Her pussy lips resting above his hard cock. He released her ear, whispering, "Ride me."

Death

Her legs quivered in anticipation. She could feel his erection pressing against her lips from her present position. Instead of getting up to straddle him, she slid her legs wide enough to accommodate him as she slid down his chest. Reaching behind her she guided him into her entrance.

The head of his large cock parted her wet lips with ease. He let her have complete control as she guided him inside her. Once he was fully inside her she used her arms to slowly rise to a seated position. The amazing sensation nearly drove her over the edge. Logan gave her first orgasm, and now she couldn't get enough. Of him, or the orgasms.

His moans drove her even closer to the edge as she began to move her hips in a rhythmic motion, bending forward to accommodate his size more easily. Logan's hips rising to meet hers creating the most delicious sensation. He rose on his elbows slightly drawing one of her breasts into his mouth.

Billie gasped as his tongue flicked across her hardened nipple. She leaned forward before grabbing for his hands and placing them on her hips. After several more strokes in this position, Billie saw stars exploding behind her eyes. Her juices flowed down both their bodies.

Slowly sitting up, never breaking the rhythm, she began to grind against him. His hips thrust deeper inside her. A quick intense orgasm hit her causing her knees to temporarily turn to jelly. Logan's strong hands were the only thing keeping her astride him.

Billie gave him a quick glare when he chuckled, "Want to switch?"

"No, I'm not finished."

"That's my tiger."

Billie reached for Logan's hands again, this time she kept going forward until she held his hands above his head. She varied thrusting and grinding, increasing her speed until the pleasure was almost too much. Logan's moans and cries joining her own. He sucked one of her breasts into his mouth. Her breast filled his mouth completely. His tongue gliding around the sensitive flesh as he sucked. The sensation sent her closer to the edge; then he bit down on the tender flesh.

The head of his cock colliding with her cervix at the same time. The orgasm smashed into her body. She ground against him tightening her pelvic muscles.

He cried out, cumming deep inside her, filling her completely. Breathing heavily, she released his hands, sitting up before sliding off his body and lying next to him.

Viper

He lay on his back, catching his breath with a huge smile on his face. "Fuck baby, that was amazing."

"Mmhmm," was all she managed.

Viper rolled up onto one elbow, looking down at his mate. "Round two?"

"No way," she laughed.

He took her hand, guiding it to his growing cock. "By the time I finish having dessert; he'll be as good as new. Ride my face baby."

"My legs don't have bones yet."

"I'll hold you up."

She smiled, kissing him before crawling over him backing her sweet juicy pussy into his face. He inhaled deeply enjoying her honeyed scent, before taking the first long slow lick, from her taint to her clit. His hands on her hips, he brought her lips down on his.

He sucked her juicy lips into his mouth, lapping up every drop of her sweet nectar off each lip, grazing his teeth on them enough to elicit a gasp from Billie. He flattened his tongue, this time he licked her from anus to clit, repeating the process several more times in slow languid motions. Occasionally lifting her hips from his face to take a breath before returning to her luscious lips.

He blew across her clit before lowering it down to his waiting lips. Viper took the engorged bud into his mouth sucking on it while he flicked his tongue across the tip. Billie smashed her pussy against his face grinding on it as he continued sucking on her clit. When he felt her close to the edge, her body tightening he bit down on the bundle of nerves. The orgasm rocked her body, he could feel her muscles contracting as he slid his fingers inside finding her g-spot. He curled his fingers, milking it to extend her orgasm. He only stopped after she collapsed, and he had to lift her off his face.

Viper positioned Billie next to him, giving her a few minutes to recover. After her breathing became normal, he shifted them so they were spooning. He lifted her hair from the back of her neck placing soft kisses along the nape of her neck.

He kissed down her spine massaging her back as he went. When he reached her ass, he kissed and nipped at each cheek before he licked her rim until she squirmed. Dipping a finger into her wetness he ran it around her rim sliding one pinky in easily she gasped and wiggled against his finger.

Viper stroked the pinky in and out of the tight rim, using his free hand to find the bottle of lube he'd hidden in the pillows earlier. Pulling his pinky out he lubed her rim and his middle finger sliding the bigger finger in. She moaned, wiggling back against him.

He continued to slide the digit in and out loosening the tight muscle. Viper inserted a second finger, Billie's moans growing increasingly louder. He began to make a scissoring motion with his fingers to stretch her more.

The more she moaned the harder his cock became. He could pound nails with it at this point, but he needed to be patient.

"Touch yourself, baby. I want to watch you while I play with your ass."

Billie's long fingers slipped down to her wetness playing along the outer folds before plunging a finger inside.

"Add another finger baby." She added a second finger, her thumb rubbing her clit. He added more lube, slipping a third finger inside her tight ass. Slowly pumping his fingers in and out of her. He spread them slowly to stretch her further. As her body drew closer to another orgasm, he stopped long enough to lube up his cock.

"Are you ready for me, babe?"

"Yes," she whimpered. Her fingers moving faster in and out of her wet channel.

He pushed the head of his cock in slowly. The sensation sending her over the top she cried out in another orgasm.

"Play with that clit. Don't stop."

Every so slowly, he worked his thick cock completely into her tight hole. He gave her time to adjust before he began thrusting his hips. Her increased moans of pleasure sent him toward his own orgasm. The wolf pushing him. His feral energy increased, and he picked up the pace, fucking her fast enough you could hear his balls slapping against her.

"Oh yes, Daddy, fuck my ass."

Her words sent him over the edge with a growl his speed increased further. His canines grew longer, and as he exploded leaving his seed deep in her ass he bit down between her neck and shoulder piercing the skin. At the same time, he opened the psychic link between them. Their bond sealed as each experienced the other's orgasms at the same time as their own.

He pulled her to him kissing the spot he bit. His softening cock was still buried in her ass when they fell asleep.

Chapter 33

Viper

"Viper wake up! Billie's gone."

He bolted upright, opening his eyes and his senses on overload. Ruby Mae stood at the end of his bed; eyes wide with fright.

"What? Tell me what happened."

"Billie and I were supposed to meet at the Laurel Valley Village store at seven-thirty this morning."

"Is it open that early?"

Ruby Mae shook her head. "I have a friend on the board that permitted us to tour the grounds during closed daylight hours. Billie used to crash in the shacks when she lived in the area. Sometimes I would run away from the orphanage and spend the night with her.

"Anyway, I arrived a few minutes late. Her bike's parked in the lot but I didn't see her. I assumed she went ahead without me. Should be easy for me to catch up in the daylight."

Ruby Mae paused drawing a deep breath, the woman becoming more upset the longer she spoke.

"Take a few deep breaths. Have a seat. I'm going to get the brothers and we'll be right back."

He didn't bother putting any clothes on since they were the only guests on the floor. Viper didn't bother to knock. He opened the door, his brothers already dressed and scarfing down donuts. Elvis cocked and brow, looking in his brother's direction.

"Ruby Mae is in my room; she says Billie is missing."

Ghost, Elvis, and Fang nearly trampled him to get across the hall. He stood there for a few seconds, mouth agape, before returning to his own room.

Ruby Mae sat in between Elvis and Fang on the love seat, while Ghost sat in the chair across from her.

His voice was gentle as he spoke. "Tell us what happened."

"Billie and I were given the green-light to go on a tour of Laurel Valley. We were supposed to meet at seven-thirty. I arrived a few minutes late and found the bike but not Billie. I searched every single outbuilding. She's not there. The only thing I found is her phone and look."

Ruby Mae pulled Billie's phone out of her pocket, opening it up she pulled up a text handing the phone to Ghost. Viper, who dressed while Ruby Mae was retelling the story, stepped up behind his brother. The text sent from Ruby Mae asked Billie to meet her at six instead, claiming she had to do something for Hervé and needed to change the time.

"I didn't send that text. Someone stole my phone. I looked for it everywhere this morning, it's why I was running behind."

"Fuck." He looked at his watch. It was nearly ten a.m., whoever had Billie had a four-hour start.

"Let's go. Ruby Mae, pick someone to ride with. Let's go find our girl."

His mind raced, who could have Billie and why? His first thought was Cayum, but they had a signed contract. One that would come with steep penalties if they broke it. Viper slid on his bike, starting it and releasing the kickstand. Ruby Mae climbed on the back of Ghost's bike, as Elvis took the lead. He was the most familiar with the area.

It took them less than five minutes to make the drive. Billie's bike is still in the lot. The place opened in less than an hour. They needed to find evidence before dozens of tourists trampled all over it.,

"Spread out and look for clues. Ruby Mae, you're with me. Can you show me where you found the phone?"

The brothers split up taking different areas of the grounds while he followed Ruby Mae to one of the old slave shacks. He could sense sorrow. It seeped into the very ground and clung to every building. Viper remembered reading about the massacre that took place on the grounds in 1887 where sixty men, women, and children of color lost their lives.

Ruby Mae led him to the edge of the bayou. "Tell me if anyone is coming, I'm going to shift and see if I can find her scent."

The redhead nodded at him; her eyes began scanning the area. It didn't take him long to turn into a massive black wolf. He let out a quick yip to his brothers before running his nose to the ground. He followed the smell from the bayou back to her bike, then quickly retraced his steps.

His brother's return yips let him know they were all doing the same thing. Finally, they had to stop. It was close to the time for sleepers to be on the grounds. They met back in the parking lot after shifting to human form.

"Any luck?" Silence greeted him, each of his brother's shaking their heads. "I lost her scent at the water's edge."

"Same," they agreed.

"I want to call Hervé to help. If anyone can find her in the bayou it will be him. I'll ask him to have someone pick up Billie's bike."

"Thanks, Ruby Mae."

An hour later, they sat in a private room at Boo's. Hervé and four other men sat around the table with them. "You say your contract with Cayum was done in the Fae court?"

"On sacred ground in the between."

"I'd say either of those should be good enough to make the Capo keep his word, yet I feel his hand in this. The boys will start searching the waters around here. There's someone else who might help us. We need to take a trip south. I have airboats waiting so we can take the bayou." He stood up nodding to his men. "You ready?"

"Locked and loaded boss."

"You boys know how to shoot? We don't have time to deal with everything *mano a mano*."

"Most of us are ex-military," Viper answered.

"Good."

Chapter 34

Viper

They loaded onto two large airboats. All of Hervé's men were armed with automatic weapons. Each of his brothers, including Fang, picked a weapon. Better to have one than not if a firefight broke out.

"Hang on, here we go."

They each took their seats as the gator started one of the big boats guiding it out onto the bayou before opening the throttle. Viper watched as the landscape blurred by them. Less than an hour later they pulled up outside a shack near Catahoula bay.

The tiny shack's front window was covered with a flag that proclaimed the occupant's redneck. Part of the roof looked like it was falling in, and the boards creaked as they left the boat, following Hervé across the rickety boardwalk that led to the shack's front door.

He turned the knob opening the door without knocking, then turned and ushered everyone inside. Once everyone was inside, he followed, closing the door behind them.

A soft noise drew his attention. Dark cloth covering a doorway pushed aside a female of unknown preternatural origin stepped out. Her multi-hued blue hair fell to her ass in waves. Blue scales cover part of her skin. Her cheeks and forehead, part of her arms and legs. She wore a Rolling Stones crop top and blue jean mini skirt that barely covered her ass. Blue-silver reptile eyes regarded their group.

"Your pops not expecting company. Not sure how happy he will be."

"Rei these are friends of mine, Viper, Elvis, Ghost, and Fang. They came down with Billie Cameron. Do you remember her?"

"That tall, dark-haired girl that went off with the Tromluí?"

"That's the one. She went missing this morning."

"That's no good. I'll wake him as soon as the sunsets. Please bring your guests in."

Hervé held open the black cloth Rei went in first, Viper and his brothers followed behind. Viper felt magic wash over him as they stepped through the door. The shack giving way to an impressive mansion.

Rei kept walking. "Please if you will follow me to the dining room. I'll have the servants whip something up while we wait."

At precisely five-thirty Rei left the room, returning less than five minutes later with a swarthy, dark-haired man in a designer suit. The vampire glided into the room effortlessly.

"Hervé, always a pleasure to see you. What brings you here?"

The gator introduced them, telling him about Billie going missing and the circumstances, then introducing the vampire as none other than Jean Lafitte.

"This is terrible," Jean said in a thick French accent. "I hate for my guests to play the waiting game. Alas, I am much quicker alone. I will search and see if I can find her."

Hervé spoke up, "We can go back up the bayou and check with my teams, while my grandfather searches."

Viper nodded, eager to do anything other than sit and wait. They loaded back onto the boat. He opened his psychic link, why the fuck hadn't he thought about it earlier.

"Billie. Can you hear me, babe? We're coming for you."

Nothing. He tried again, each time he met with silence. Either she couldn't hear him, or she wasn't answering. He had to go with the first, knowing she'd answer him if she could.

"I marked Billie last night. I can't reach her through our bond."

"The mate's mark?" Hervé asked.

"Yes."

"Only a few beings around here powerful enough to block a mate's mark."

They spent the rest of the night going up and down the bayou. Hervé even turned into gator form and swam the bayou looking for her with the rest of his men. Mentally exhausted by the time dawn came, they wearily returned to the vampire's shack.

Jean waited for them in the salon, sipping form a crystal goblet no doubt filled with blood. He looked up when they came in. "I'm afraid I had no luck. I'll continue searching tomorrow night. Please feel free to stay here if you need. The sun's up soon."

They spent two more days looking for Billie; on the third day Mother arrived with Ava. The girl insisted on coming down when she heard Billie went missing. The pink-haired bit of fluff bounced into the vampire's house, throwing her arms around him hugging his legs until he picked her up. Viper looked to his brother. "She was safer back in Oklahoma."

"Mother told me that, but I came to help. I can see things the others can't."

Chapter 35

Death

Billie paced the cell for the thousandth time. She went to meet Ruby Mae. Her friend told her all about the contract Viper and his brothers made with Cayum. Including telling Cayum that she now belonged to him. Heartbroken, she ran toward the slave shacks.

She never minded the restless spirits that roamed the grounds. Billie spent most nights in one of the plantation buildings. Switching buildings every night, making sure she left no trace come first light. Billie wasn't paying attention; for the first time in her life, her guard was down.

Cayum waited for her by the bayou with an obsidian witch. The witch sucked out enough of her energy with one touch that Billie lost consciousness. When she regained consciousness, she was in a cell. Three times a day someone shoved food through a slot at the bottom of the door. She had a cot with a threadbare blanket, a single bare light hanging from the ceiling, a sink, and a toilet. For three long days, she thought of ways to get out. So far nothing she tried worked.

Suddenly the door opened, the bright light from the hall blinding her temporarily. A figure pushed through the door before it slammed and locked. Billie stood up off the bed ready to fight if necessary.

"I'm not here to hurt you," a soft voice said.

Billie stepped out of the shadows to inspect the visitor. She was a few inches shorter, with ebony skin. Her long dark hair in box braids with gold accents in the braids. What stood out most about the casually dressed woman was her stunning blue eyes. They were the color of the waters of Ambergris Caye in Belize. Recognition dawned in her head.

"Merci?"

"*Oui*. You have me at a disadvantage. You seem to know who I am, yet I have no idea who you are."

"Billie Cameron," she offered her hand to the other woman.

Merci took Billie's hand in hers holding on to it after she shook it. Billie watched as the blue of her iris bled into her pupil, becoming solid blue. Her eyes started shifting like moving water. Waves crashing, Billie fell into her gaze much as she had done Lance's, only, this time, she wasn't afraid.

She didn't know how long Merci delved into her mind. Eventually, she pulled back, returning Billie to the present. Memories of Logan flooded into her mind. Him teaching her to fight, bringing her food and clothes. Then he disappeared. She stayed around for two weeks before leaving the area, tired of dealing with the gangs and fighting the boys.

"You removed the block."

"Yes, but there's so much more you don't know."

"Like what?"

"Like how to unlock your wings."

"My wings?"

"The tattoo on your back is not a tattoo. Now that your memory is whole, the time will come soon for you to use your powers."

"How do I unlock them? How will I know?"

"I do not have either answer, I'm afraid."

"We, my mate and I, spoke to Lance. He hoped we'd find you."

"Some goons grabbed me a few weeks ago. I've been down here ever since."

"Where is here?"

"A hidden underground temple in Lake Salvador."

Viper

He didn't like Ava being there, but she had a point. They sat in the dining room in the late afternoon "sun". All light inside the house was magical so Jean could run around without worrying about actual sunlight frying him.

He and his brothers were piecing together the riddle. Once it was in front of them, they passed it around for Hervé, Ava, Rei, and Jean to see.

Rei spoke first, "Jean has a rare flower in the garden that only blooms once a year. It lasts for a few hours."

"Yes, if we change the lighting in the arboretum, we can induce it to bloom early. That would fulfill tomorrow's dead part of the riddle."

"What about the block?"

"I think it might refer to the magickal block on mine and Billie's memory. Wolf broke through mine with some help."

"What about Billie's?"

"She needs Merci Laveau to unlock hers."

"When's the last time you tried your mate bond?" Ghost asked.

"Not since the first day she went missing."

"Try again."

Viper closed his eyes focusing on his mate. *"Billie, can you hear me, love?"*

"Logan?"

"Yes, it's me. Are you all right?"

"I'm fine. I found Merci."

"Did she remove your block?"

"Yes."

"Do you know where you are?"

"An underground temple, beneath Lake Salvador."

"I'll figure a way to find you. Stay strong. I love you."

"I love you."

"She's in a temple under Lake Salvador with Merci."

"Ahh," Hervé said, "I believe I understand the rest of the riddle. The door to the underground temple will appear when the moon rises."

Chapter 36

Viper

They gathered onto the boats as the moon rose heading toward the middle of the lake. Lake Salvador was a shallow lake with an average depth of around six feet. The airboat skimmed over the surface closing the distance as the moon's light began to shine on the water.

He watched as a stone archway and steps rose from the water. When the boat stopped, Hervé leaped onto the stone steps first, motioning for him to follow. Viper had the petals of the Queen of Night flower in his hand.

"What about the towers?"

The gator king smiled. "I am the croc. The towers are the ridges in my gator form.

"Start at my head and count the different colored ridges. There will be four distinct sections of off-colored ridges. That's the code to unlock the door."

"Just one question: how did you get the key, or rather wind up being the key?"

"It passes down from ruler to ruler."

"Got it."

Hervé shifted into his impressive gator form. Over twenty feet in length by the time he finished shifting. Viper quickly counted the odd colored ridges. 7-23-13-9. He touched the numbers on the stone pad. The door slid silently open. He waited for the gator to shift back to human form before starting through the door.

Before he could step through, a hand on his shoulder stopped him. "The pookah needs to go first. Fae can see the unseen. She'll be able to spot any invisible traps."

Reluctantly, he retrieved Ava from the boat, staying close behind her as she entered. Hervé, Jean, and his brothers followed. Rei was staying behind with the boat and the bodyguards.

When Ava reached the bottom step, she let out a shrill scream. Just a step behind her he saw nothing, yet when he stepped down, he felt a chill run up his spine. Fear pulsed all around him. He recognized it, dragon fear. The temple was well guarded indeed.

He knelt beside Ava. "It's not real. It's like a spell."

"What is it?" the girl whispered trembling."

"Dragon fear." He said it loud enough for the others to hear, then he bent down, picking Ava up and carrying her down the hall.

"Stop! There's a trap."

He stopped. "What is it?"

"Swinging blades. Can you put me down?"

"You will not try and go through."

"I wasn't planning to. I'm a kid, I'm not stupid."

He let her down a small smile tugging at the corner of his mouth. Her feistiness reminded him of Billie.

"What's the last line of the riddle?" she asked.

"Count the pure and silent knock."

"It's a heartbeat," Mother said, coming to stand next to them in the wide stone hall. Braziers lit in intervals along the wall offered dim lighting. Though none of them had issues seeing in low light, or darkness for that matter.

"I'll go first. Ava, can you walk me through it?"

"Yes."

Viper watched as Mother stepped forward until the rock beneath him gave off a faint glow. He paused, waiting for Ava to give him the go-ahead. Mother followed the young girl's directions making it safely to the other side.

One by one they followed until they reached Jean, who didn't have a heartbeat. He picked Ava up, carrying her through the trap using her heartbeat and keeping the little girl from making the walk alone.

They spent another twenty minutes walking down twisting hallways. Eventually, the halls led to a large room with cavernous ceilings. A large dais sat on the far end of the room. On top of the dais sat a black marble and onyx, boxy structure not unlike the drawings he'd seen of the l'Arche des Morts.

He halted mid-step scenting the air. "Demon."

Viper drew Ava with him into the shadows. Not ten seconds later, Yannich entered the room from the opposite side accompanied by Cayum, the obsidian witch, and a few goons. He swore under his breath.

Cayum stopped in front of the ark, turning to address Yannich. "You say that one of your men spotted the pookah near Thibodaux yesterday."

"Yes, master. Everything is going as planned. We should have the Fae girl in our custody before the moon's eclipse."

"Good, good. I'll be back before the eclipse. Don't let me down."

"I won't master. You can count on me."

It was all he could do not to go after the Dark Fae and rip his head off, price be damned, but he needed to find his mate first. Then he needed to get everyone out of here safely, including the ark.

They decided to split up in teams after the demon left the area. Fang and Hervé went one direction. He, Ava, and Mother went another direction, while Ghost and Elvis took a third.

Death

The door to their cell opened surprising her. She instantly went on guard stepping in front of Merci.

"Death are you in here?"

She recognized Fang's voice. Thrilled to see him she enveloped him in a quick hug.

He returned the hug then grabbed her hand. "Let's get out of here."

Billie stepped around Fang to embrace Hervé. "Thank you."

"Always savin' that tail, now ain't I girl?"

She laughed. "Yeah, I guess that's true."

"Ma belle fille, tu es de la famille, non?"

"Oui. I finally understand what family is. I'm sorry I didn't figure it out when you were trying to show me."

"Les petites sœurs font des erreurs."

She laughed, "Way more than my share it seems. We better go before Cayum or that witch comes back."

"What kind of witch?"

"Obsidian."

"Merde."

Merci stepped softly out of the shadows. Her solid blue eyes glowed with power. "If we run into the witch, I'll take care of her."

Billie quickly introduced everyone before Hervé led them out of the dungeon, and back toward the temple's main room. Sounds of fighting reached her ears as they turned the corner.

"Let's go," she said, itching to kick some ass.

The brothers were engaged in battle with Cayum's goons and from the looks of it several members of the Swamp Devils. Billie took a few seconds to size up the battle before choosing a jackal shifter. She had experience fighting them and knew their weaknesses.

Fuckers always attacked in packs. Well, she was going single out this motherfucker. Running into the fray she clocked the jackal in the jaw knocking his head back.

"Come on Swamp RAT, show me whatcha got." For the first time in her life, she was the provoker, the attacker. No longer would she be a victim, just defending herself.

The jackal turned on her snapping his jaws at her face, but she was quick. She danced a few steps back drawing the jackal with her. Perfect white teeth showed as she gave her opponent a genuine smile. Billie was going to enjoy kicking his ass, fighting for her family. Fighting with her family.

A confused look crossed the jackal's face at her smile. Keeping the smile on her face, she side-kicked his knee in a brutal downward motion. A satisfying pop told her she broke his knee. The jackal went down howling, cradling his knee. That break would take him a few hours to heal. Should put him out of the fight.

They were outnumbered four to one at the moment. Billie intended to try and incapacitate her opponents as quickly as possible.

She didn't bother looking to see how her family fared; instinctively knowing each one could hold their own. Billie sized up the nearest opponent, a sleeper by the looks of him. He didn't give off any energy signatures like other preternaturals.

His back to her, she managed to get behind him and put him in a headlock before he knew what hit. He struggled against her, but she had the superior strength, not to mention technique. Once she choked him out, she quickly applied enough pressure to the carotid to keep him knocked out. Using a dim mak technique she learned overseas to interrupt the flow of chi through his body.

She continued to single out opponents, taking them down as quickly as possible. Some were quick while others took several minutes. Her mimic powers taking on other powers at an unprecedented rate. Billie lost count of the number of opponents she fought and eventually incapacitated.

A scream of pain took her attention away from choosing her next opponent. Billie turned toward the scream. Fang lay on the floor, Yannich stood over his body. His arm and hand formed into an obsidian dagger, blood dripping off it. She ran faster than she ever had; plowing into the demon, she knocked him back several feet. Immediately, she dropped to her knees in front of Fang. Blood dripped from his mouth, the life fading from his eyes.

No! This is not happening. I will not lose my brother. Something within her shifted. Warm energy enveloped her. Billie slammed her hands onto Fang's chest. "YOU WILL NOT DIE! DO YOU HEAR ME?" Golden light shot from her hands into Fang's body.

Suddenly she was airborne. Yannick regained his footing. He picked her up and tossed her across the room. She landed with a thud into the wall. It only served to piss her off. The demon stood over Fang's body, one hand shaping into the dagger again. Once formed, he slashed into the air. The other hand making sigils as he changed. An inky rip began to form above Fang's body.

Oh no, you don't motherfucker. Rage consumed her as the images of every foul deed Yannick committed flashed in her mind.

With each image her power grew, the portal ever widening. Battle all around her. She got to her feet running toward Yannick. An audible pop and she was airborne, but by her own power this time, hurtling toward him as large black feathered wings sprouted from her back.

Billie grabbed a hold of Yannick, taking them both through the portal.

Chapter 37

Viper

He knew Billie joined the fray at some point, he felt her presence. Viper was engaged in battle with three other shifters when he heard the scream. He wanted to investigate but couldn't afford to glance away for even a second.

Viper sent a quick thought to his mate, *you okay.* While she didn't respond with words. He could feel her anger. It reverberated down the thread that connected them fueling the anger in his wolf.

The few second distractions cost him as one of the demon wolves from the Swamp Demons sliced with razor-sharp claws leaving bloody gashes down his chest. Viper roared using the anger from Billie to fuel his alpha power he pushed the anger outward. The energy knocking his opponents back.

He used the opportunity to grab the demon wolf by the throat. As he brought the shifter in, he punched through his chest; breaking his ribcage he pulled out his still-beating heart. With the link to Billie still open he'd seen some of the shifters past deeds. In retribution for what he'd done, Viper crushed the beating heart in his hands. He growled at the other two, howling as he dove into them.

Fury rode his body until all that lay around him was the unconscious or parts of fallen foes. He'd ripped off limbs, and heads. Each time a few of the deeds they'd done flashed before his eyes.

Viper paused taking in the scene around him. He searched quickly taking note of his brothers. When he saw Fang laying on the floor with Ava kneeling by his side, a strange portal to one side, he sprinted across the room shifting into human form as he arrived.

Fang lay in a pool of blood his face drained of color. His eyes were barely open. Viper felt for his pulse. Weak but steady. He took his hand, "Fang, can you tell me what happened?"

The others gathered around them as the pup struggled to speak. Fang lifted his arm pointing to the portal. "Billie."

Viper started through the portal, but several sets of hands grabbed him when Merci shouted, "WAIT!"

"Your link: check it. Is she hurt or in pain?"

Viper quickly checked the link he left open to his mate. He didn't feel anything but rage, only the energy transformed into a righteous rage.

"She's finding out who she is," he whispered. Tears of joy and a little fear on her behalf coursed down his face.

"Pussy," Fang whispered hoarsely.

The absurdity of Fang calling him a pussy made him burst out laughing. Belly shaking, well ab-shaking, belly laughter.

He knelt back beside the pup. "Kid, you have so much to learn. Merci, can you help him?"

Viper watched the beautiful woman approach Fang. She looked around twenty, yet the power that radiated around her said she was much older. A century or more if he had to guess.

Merci knelt beside Fang, the blue in her striking eyes bleeding into the pupil until it disappeared. She held her hands above his chest moving around to take in his wound. He dated a healer before. Viper asked Tessa incessant questions about her healing powers. Less than a century old at the time, he'd been more pup than man.

Blue energy poured from her hands sinking down into Fang's chest before spilling out and encompassing his entire body. Fang's body smoothly morphed into a large golden-brown wolf, then, just as smooth, he shifted into combat form before returning to human form. The blue energy receded and Merci sat back, breathing heavily from the exertion.

"Changing him was the best way to restore his heart to complete health. Billie closed the hole in his heart, or he would have bled out."

She patted the boy on his shoulder before sitting down completely. "You, my dear pup, are the catalyst our angel needed."

"Billie's an angel?"

Death

"You made a grave mistake little girl," Yannich snarled, shedding his human skin for his true grotesque form. More than seven feet tall with cloven hooves and smooth red skin. Large spikes protruded from his knees and elbows. Two massive horns curled around his head like a ram's. Giant six-inch fangs showed when the demon opened its mouth.

"You're the one that's made the mistake, Noszal'toth."

The demon recoiled at his real name being spoken aloud. Billie stepped forward, her wings unfurling again. Deep black feathers, like looking into the void, tinged with blood red. With each step she took, the red increased, the black slowly being consumed by it.

She stopped a few feet away when he started laughing at her. He pointed to her wings; thick red droplets fell from her semi-relaxed wings. Each one hit sizzling and popping on the unholy ground.

"You're an angel, in hell. Do you think you have any power over me here?" He burst out laughing again. "Half a dozen imps could clean your clock down here."

An eerie smile crept across her face; her lips curled into a snarl before settling into a brilliant beaming smile. "Not if your father's name is Michael."

A gleaming sword engulfed in black and red fire appeared in her hands. She charged the demon, who didn't have time to forge his own blade or dodge out of the way. The blade sliced a thin line across his chest, causing the demon to cry out in pain as the holy flame charred his flesh.

Billie knew in that instant she could have cut off his head, sending him to his final death, but she wasn't done punishing him. Not by far. This demon made far too many transgressions on the mortal plane. Noszal'toth grew fifteen feet tall, grabbing her before hurling her across the hellish landscape. Her body still in motion when she hit the ground, Billie tumbled, ending on her knees. The jagged rocks cut through her jeans. She extended her wings, which acted like a parachute slowing, then stopping her slide.

A twenty-foot trail of blood was left where the sharp black rocks sliced her knees. When Billie stood up, bits of rocks fell away showing shiny black knees where the flesh had once been. She shot up into the air before swiftly descending on the demon, sword drawn.

The demon managed to block her strike, but the blow brought him to his knees. She brought her sword back pounding it into his blade arm repeatedly. Taking chips out of the stone with each blow. He was near cowering by the time she relented. Instinctively, she knew it was an act.

When he laughed and sprung forward, she dodged, dropped to the ground, and brought her blade up into his gut. Pressing the blade in as far as it would go, thick black blood ran down her hand. Billie sliced down, spilling the demon's insides, outside.

Taking a few steps back, she watched him drop to the ground writhing in pain.

"Kill me, you can't leave me in agony. You're an angel."

Billie laughed, "I'm an avenging angel. We're cut from a different cloth. Had I the time, I'd sit and watch you suffer for the next decade before I took your head."

"I'll heal long before that," the demon wheezed.

"You can't heal from a holy wound demon, not this one."

"No! It can't be, you're supposed to be dead."

"What do you mean?"

"If I'm dying, I'll take you out with me. At least my name will be sung throughout the land."

"What are you talking about?"

"You'll never know," the demon said, cackling, pulling out a dark orb.

It pulsed with evil. She didn't know what it was, just that it was not good. When he tossed it toward the portal Billie dove to intercept it. She managed to get in front of the orb, using the blade like a bat to knock it away from the portal.

Billie knew the moment she fucked up.

The orb exploded, the force throwing her back through the portal. Holding the sword up high, the energy expanded into a protective dome over the inhabitants of the room. A ball of black fire and rock washed over the dome.

Dozens of demons began to escape from the rip caused by the explosion. Billie could do nothing but watch helplessly as the black fire continued to pound against the dome for several more minutes.

The concussive boom that followed knocked her unconscious. Strong arms wrapped around her as the world faded.

Chapter 38

Viper

He opened his eyes slowly, what freight train hit him. Then memories came flooding back into his mind. His eyes sprang open the rest of the way. *Whew.* Billie lay still in his arms through his link he knew she was only unconscious and not injured.

Viper scanned the area quickly assessing the damage. His brothers, including Fang, were slowly getting to their feet. Merci sat up, shaking her head. Little Ava held Billie's sword in her hands, the dome still active. Demons still poured out of the rip.

"We've got to close the rip."

Hervé walked up to the brother's phone in hand. "I'm afraid it's worse than that. We've been unconscious for several hours, and the paranormal world is no longer a secret."

Fang came over. "I've got her, brother, you go check out the pictures our gator friend has."

"Thank you."

He gently laid Billie in his brother's lap then headed to Hervé. The rest of the brothers and Jean stood in a loose circle around him. The taller man handed him the phone; Viper began to scroll through the pics. Ten minutes later, he'd read all the texts Hervé's team had sent, before thinking to check his own. Each of the brothers had texts from other members of the wolves including Blade, and he had one from Omen.

"You have the answer you seek, but you've got to let her go."

He wanted to send Omen a follow-up text asking what the hell that meant, but he knew their leader would have given him any additional information he had.

Viper looked at each face, "Anyone have any ideas? How do we put the cat back in the box?"

"How many hours until Dawn?" Ghost asked.

"Less than hours until the sun rises," Jean replied. "Let us get back to the shack. I have books there that might give us the answer. Ava, can you keep up the barrier long enough to get us to the shack?"

"Yes, I think so. At least I can keep the demons away from us while we get to your place."

"Good girl."

It took them fifteen minutes to get through enough of the rubble to get up the stairs and back to the boat. Viper let out a sigh of relief when he saw the shield had protected Rei and the others as well.

Jean glided to the young woman's side wrapping her up. "I'll explain on the way."

Rei nodded. He let the pup carry his mate out. The boy might be permanently attached to their hip. Once they arrived at the shack Fang asked to carry Billie to her room. He insisted on watching after his guardian angel until she woke up.

Billie might sleep for another few hours or the rest of the night. She absorbed the worst of the blast and protected everyone else in the process. Her power would undoubtedly grow now that it was unlocked.

Jean led them to a large three-story library. The shelves were lined with ancient books. Viper scanned them looking for prophecy and time travel. Mother and Ghost joined him while Elvis and Hervé started with ancient magicks. Jean and Rei headed to the books he had on the Occult. Merci and Ava disappeared into the kitchen. Ava needed to refuel after expending that much power.

Ava

Ava followed the directions Rei gave her into the kitchen. She needed to refuel, and she also needed to convince Merci to sneak her back into the temple. Food first, her stomach reminded her with a loud growl.

She heard Merci chuckle. "My, your stomach is not shy, little one."

Ava smiled. "I'm a growing girl. Do you know how to cook? I'm not so good."

"I sure do. If we had time, I'd make you the best gumbo you ever had. I sense our time is short. Am I wrong, little one?"

Ava looked up at Merci, the seer's eyes had gone all blue. "No, you're not," she whispered.

"No fret petite, I'll get you fueled up and fit as a fiddle in no time. I best figure we got an hour, no?"

"About that, yes. Thanks for making this easy."

"'Tis only easy because you are unknown to me and I know 'tis for the greater good."

"You'll take me back to the temple?"

"I will after I feed you; let's go make you a proper Cajun feast."

Merci kept the conversation casual as she whipped up dish after dish of Cajun-inspired food: shrimp omelets, crawfish pasta with thick chunks of pancetta, and fresh-shucked peas; mushroom five cheese pizza and beignets with chocolate sauce for dessert.

"Can you help me find a pen and paper? I want to leave a note behind for Billie."

"*Petit bonbon*, you are going to break even my heart."

Sometime later they crept out of the shack. Ava headed toward the end of the pier. When they arrived, Merci grabbed her hand leading her down a set of stairs to the dock. Ava couldn't believe her eyes when she spotted two enormous gators laying on the end of the dock.

Merci didn't slow down, she didn't stop until they were at the gator's tail. "Okay girls move a bit so we can get on. Ava, slide your arms around her and hang on."

Ava watched Merci and then mimicked her. The cold water shocked her for a second, causing her to nearly let go.

She adjusted to the cool water, enjoying the unique ride. Ava hated saying goodbye to Billie. The angel had been through so much to protect her. Now it was her turn to protect the woman she loved beyond measure.

Once they reached the gate, Merci helped her get back into the chamber where the ark had been before the explosion. Who knows where it was now? It didn't matter. She was here to play her part in the prophecy. Something she'd known since birth.

Ava took in the scene making her way to the rift, there at the bottom's edge, a small bit of the original portal remained. She felt Merci's hand rub her ears soothingly before stepping away. Ava closed her eyes concentrating her small body and began to grow smaller until only a small white rabbit with pale pink eyes remained.

She hopped through the portal finding a chunk of rock large enough to hide what she knew was to come.

Chapter 39

Billie

"You'll never know," the demon said, cackling, pulling out a dark orb.

It pulsed with evil. She didn't know what it was, just that it was not good. When he tossed it toward the portal Billie dove to intercept it...

A small white ball of fur caught her attention too late, she tripped, falling back through the portal. Her body collided with her mate's.

"I've got you, babe."

Billie pulled in her wings, ready to launch back through the portal when she saw Ava on the other side, holding the black orb in her small hands.

"AVA!" she yelled as time began to slow down.

The pookah's white ears began to glow the same pink as her hair. The ball expanded until Billie could barely see her. She tried to move but her body wouldn't cooperate. The black orb exploded, blowing pink energy everywhere.

"Noo!" Suddenly her body could move, and Billie ran to the portal trying to reach it before it closed completely. She couldn't lose Ava. When the portal closed in front of her, Billie fell to her knees, sobbing.

"Why? Why did it have to be Ava, she's an innocent child."

Bille felt her mate's arms around her once again, only this time he was joined by the brothers, each one putting their arms around her until she was in the middle of them. They let her sob until she was too exhausted to go on, then Fang surprised her, asking if he could carry her up the stairs back to the boat.

Viper, Mother, Elvis, and Ghost carried the ark up the stairs. Billie wasn't as shocked as she should have been to find the vampires, she'd met the first night waiting for them with a boat of their own.

"Can you take me to the boat while the rest of the brothers deal with them?"

Fang laughed. "Of course, my lady. I would take you anywhere you want to go."

"Thank you."

Once they were on the boat, she laid her head on Fang's shoulder, falling into an exhausted sleep.

Viper

Billie began to stir a few miles from the Dansereau House. Viper had kept the third floor rented out. In his heart, he knew his mate would be back. He didn't know it would be under such gut-wrenching circumstances.

"We're almost to Thibodaux, love. Would you like a hot bath? Maybe some food?"

"I'd love a bath, but I'm not really hungry."

Viper picked his mate up in his arms as soon as the boat slid up to the dock. He carried her to the house and up to the third floor laying her on the bed before heading to the tub and drawing her a bath. He added bubbles and turned on the jets for a few seconds to make extra.

After turning off the water, he retrieved Billie from the bed, helping her undress and slip into the tub.

"Do you want me to stay?"

She shook her head. "I need to be alone."

He bent down, brushing his lips across her forehead. "I love you. I'll be in the other room if you need me.

Viper sat down on the loveseat sending off quick texts to his brothers before checking his text message. A soft knock at the door had him up and across the room, Merci and Lance Laveau stood on the other side.

"May we come in?"

"Of course, please come in. Have a seat, Billie is in the tub."

"We'd like to wait," Merci said.

"We have the information we want to give both of you," Lance added.

Viper understood. "Let's give her a few minutes with her thoughts."

They spent the next twenty minutes making polite small talk while Billie soaked in the tub. She came out wrapped in his thick terry cloth robe. Billie sat on his lap after saying hello to Lance and Merci.

"We're sorry to bother you," Merci said, "I have something for you from Ava."

She handed Billie a bright pink envelope with a white bunny sticker on it. Fresh tears slid down his mate's face as she clutched the envelope to her chest.

"Read it when you're ready. There is no rush. My brother brought it to my attention that you need the second half of the riddle."

Lance pulled out a linen envelope handing it to him. Viper opened the envelope taking out the letter before unfolding it and holding it so they could both read it.

An angel sent to avenge the wrongs will find love in the arms of a wolf.

When two worlds collide, a child will sacrifice it all to awaken the father of fangs.

Hate spilled red on the ground will awaken Him in a rage, all will be doomed. Humanity lost.

Love spilled red on the lips will awaken Him in divinity. Humanity saved.

Two daughters of a Goddess, one dark one light, will be split at birth. Never knowing the other until they meet their fated mates.

When Odin's own rise to protect their mother, twins will lead the charge, slaying the serpent and its minions.

THE END

Epilogue

Viper

Viper watched his wife, round with their first child, twins, finish off her fourth soft-shelled parmesan crab. It took them eighteen months to get back to Thibodaux, but here they were sitting in the private room at Boo's surrounded by family.

After Ava's death, he and Billie stayed at the Dansereau House for another month. Eventually, Billie opened Ava's letter. Which simply said:

I love you, mom. I'll be back someday.

Three days ago, he received the approval letter for his death claim on Cayum from the Dark Fae tribunal. Now he had only to deal with the Tromluí boss. He had the Elvis' part of the contract stricken immediately. The Fae agreed because of the serious nature of Cayum's breach.

About Candi Fox

I could go on for hours about anyone, but me. True fact. :) I'm a glamazon author with multi-hued hair and a heart bigger than Texas with a deep love of animals and the supernatural. I find inspiration everywhere. I collided with the supernatural world at the age of 2. My first specter. An abandoned bridge becomes the home of a troll, or maybe a gateway to some faraway world. Turtles in a pond spawn an entire YA series. I live in the SouthWest/ish :) with my husband, 3 rabbits, 3 dogs, 2 cats, and 2 horses.
I write because the stories stalk me until I put them on paper. I once had a werewolf tell me, "I not a fucking vampire." Meaning he didn't care to talk on a personal level. Sex is the exception of that one. I write PNR, PNR Mystery & Thriller, HEA, 80's, Old West with a TWIST. Historical Old West Collides with Magic, Madness, and a touch of Steam Punk. Oh, and did I mention it's mostly going to be Reverse Harem. I'll let you guess my inspiration for that genre. *wink*

I hope you invite me in and let me transport you away.

Connect with Candi Fox online, she loves to hear from you:
https://midnightcandi.com/
https://www.facebook.com/CandiFox01
https://www.facebook.com/CandiFoxAuthor/
https://www.instagram.com/candimfox/
https://twitter.com/CandiFox?lang=en
https://amzn.to/2IriXGw
https://bit.ly/2Jihkw4
https://www.bookbub.com/authors/candi-fox
https://www.facebook.com/groups/foxyfanatics/
https://www.facebook.com/groups/paranormalhunger/
Pinterest https://www.pinterest.com/candifox1/

Other Books by Candi Fox

Killing Chronicles Series
Strange Beginnings
Sweet Obsession
Twisted Time

Naked Truth Series
Harlequin's Deception
Witch's Transformation
Solstice
Stand Alone Series
Pendale High (Not YA)
Savanna James
Lennon Cooper

Odin's Wolves MC
Half-God, Half-Wolf, All Bad Ass
Rage
Viper
Coming Soon
Blade

www.ingramcontent.com/pod-product-compliance
Lightning Source LLC
Chambersburg PA
CBHW071405150726
48000CB00001B/170